Original title, *De reis*
Published by Free Musketeer

The Trip to Valariru

Zoe Toet

America Star Books
Frederick, Maryland

Softcover 9781681226279
PUBLISHED BY AMERICA STAR BOOKS, LLLP
www.americastarbooks.com
Frederick, Maryland

We dive into the story!

Kellie and Gaya

What's wrong with Latrez?

"Hooo, hallelujah, stop for a moment!" Kellie pulled on the reins of her horse.

"What?!" asked Gaya surprised as she jumped from her horse.

"I think there was something wrong with Latrez. Look at her face. She looks weary." Kellie pointed at Gaya's horse Latrez, indeed there was something seriously wrong.

"What's wrong with Latrez?" Kellie again asked Gaya in a serious tone.

"She's a little tired, I think yes, but those two kilometers are just short," said Gaya, because she really did not want to walk.

"Gaya! There is really something wrong, "said Kellie.

"But what?" Asked Gaya now worried and stared at Latrez's head. She looked tired and clumsy.

"Maybe it needs some water," said Kellie and walked to the river. Kellie grabbed her water pad that hung from her pocket, and filled it to the brim with ditch water.

"Kel, that water is dirty," said Gaya.

"There's nothing for Latrez if you notice," said Kellie and gave the water cushion.

Gaya took it and took off the cap and poured it in Latrez's mouth. The water lapped inside, you could hear slurping, and the water also drove past her foot on the ground.

"Is it drinking or spitting the water?" Asked Kellie.

"Haha, very funny Kel. Latrez does not drool." Suddenly Lily pranced actively.

"Quiet, quiet, so we go riding again," Kellie said soothingly to her horse, grabbed the reins and stroked Lily's nose.

"Shall we go again?" Asked Gaya.

"Yeah, okay, I think Latrez is also good now," nodded Kellie and looked at Latrez. She looked
better. But Kellie did not noticed that the saddle was drawn tight with Latrez and Lily, such that it hurt the animals.

"Okay, we can go," said Kellie, jumped on her horse, and they drove off.

LILY!

"A beautiful day," Kellie looked outside her window, "I have to go make breakfast!" Kellie told herself.

"Gaya is still in bed, and the youngest will make the food. What stupid rule is that?" Hissed Kellie, and made a fist of her hand.

"Well look at you, youngest still learning the ropes," Kellie imitated Gaya with a niggling voice, "shit," she muttered and dived back into her bed, as a protest.

But when she heard rumbling outside she muttered, "Gaya, I really don't know how to make breakfast, but I just go look because I hear strange noises!" she ended suddenly anxious, stood on tiptoe and looked through her window.

"Lily" Kellie saw a figure in dark clothes pulling a rope on Lily while the horse struggled a bit. She began to whinny in anger. Kellie ran to the hallway and fumbled at the front door.

"Shit, locked," she complained, took the key out of the closet and hastily put the key into the keyhole. The door flung open with a bang, and slammed into the wall. Kellie rushed to Lily and pushed the boy aside.

"What are you doing with my horse?" She cried and pulled the rope out of the black boy's glove. He got frightened that he suddenly ran away.

"So, that's gone." Kellie stroked Lily's nose and neck, "you're safe again. What a scary figure was say!" At the same time Gaya came walking.

"What is going on here? And more importantly, where is the breakfast?!"

"Sorry Mom, ehh... Gaya," muttered Kellie, "I was just so enjoying myself without parents."

"You have to stick to the rules," said Gaya.

Gaya and Kellie were 11 and 12 years old. Their parents left on summer holidays and left them together in their grandparents' summer house.

"You are really like my mother! Gaya you know what nearly had just happened?!" Kellie said pissed.

"Yes, what happened then?" Asked Gaya seriously she stroke Latrez.

"A boy in black tried to peck Lily!"

"Get?"

"Yes, steal."

"Oh, okay, then it's good."

"Good? Good? Are you *out* of your *mind?*" Exclaimed Kellie offended. "If your horse would have been taken, you won't stop talking about it all day!" She screamed through the whole village.

"I meant," Gaya said quietly, "pecking is not a nice word."

"Very easy to say," Kellie squeezed her eyes, she tied Lily's the rope back to the post. She turned and walked to the house feeling pissed.

"What's wrong with her?" Gaya asked Latrez.

Latrez whinnied and bent over a few blades of grass, and ate it. Her horse began to prance occasionally, just like that.

Gaya lifted her eyebrow and thought that it was indeed a strange story of Lily being kidnapped. Latrez was still nervous.

"You stay here Latrez, take it easy, there's nothing wrong. I'm going home."

When Gaya walked home Kellie was just about to go back to Lily, which was still out on the pole stuck behind the shed.

"Come Lily, I don't trust that man for no horse turd." Kellie just wanted to jump on her horse when it moved. Ting, ting, ting, ting, ting!

"That is Gaya's song, why are they calling me now?" Muttered Kellie, and put her mobile phone to her ear. She walked back home towards Gaya.

"Kellie! Come quickly, Latrez is gone!"

"What?!"

"Where is she?" Kellie looked around anxiously.

"Away," Gaya sobbed and she burst into tears.

"Who was it?" Kellie looked worried.

"I don't know, but Lily, where is she?"

"In the sands. Lily!" suddenly Kellie was worried. She ran with beating heart to the dark shed.

Lily was gone. Not to the pole, not in the shed. "No! Not Lily, too!"

Gaya ran to the shed tense. It was empty, there was only a little straw. "Ooh," Gaya hit her hands to her face, "what now?"
"What is wrong with you? Normally you would cry. We have to find them! Come on!" Kellie put her hand around Gaya," everything will be fine, I mean it. We need to start looking!"

"You're right, we have to be strong, we'll go," said Gaya, stood up and walked down the road to the bus stop, she waved to Kellie.

Kellie smiled, ran to Gaya, and went next to her on the bench at the bus stop. "The bus is there," said Gaya. She stood up and waved her arms.

"He can see us really well," said Kellie, "it's not a taxi."

The bus honked and stopped in front of the bus stop, he pressed a button and all the doors were opened. Gaya and Kellie boarded the bus. The bus honked again and the doors were closed.

"Sir, will this go to the city?" Asked Kellie and walked to the gentleman.

"Yes, what do you think?" Said the driver grumpy.

"Sorry, I did not know you were angry." Kellie put five euro
the hand of the bus driver, got two tickets and some change back and walked to a bench near the back,. Gaya sat beside her.

"Well?" She asked, "Is it going to town?"

Kellie nodded. "Nice."

"Why do you really want to go to the city? Do you think our horses can be found there? You're not shopping in town?!" muttered Kellie.

"No duh! We go around asking if anyone has seen our horses. Maybe Linda or so, maybe Jessy saw him, or John, who still lives in the city? Or Jan? Leon, perhaps Ba..."

"Yes, yes, okay, well, I understand," Kellie looked out.

"What's got into you?"

"Yes, hello do I have to explain? Our horses are gone!

You are acting strange. You act as if you don't care that Latrez and Lily were gone!"

"That I care!" Gaya shouted angrily.

"Well you don't."

Gaya turned. Kellie scowled and looked out the window, then she began to sob softly. Gaya heard it but did nothing. Gaya was also crying a little. The bus stopped a while later.

"We are here, will someone get out?" Asked the driver unkindly.

Gaya and Kellie got out. There were still a few people on the bus that remained.

Then something happened that the girls did not expect. The driver pulled out a camera and took their photo. He smiled mysteriously and put the camera back in the crate next to him and turned the key next to the steering wheel again, the engine growled, the driver turned the wheel. The bus drove away.

"Shall we go to Linde?" Gaya asked.

"All right," Gaya and Kellie walked to a girl who was standing with her back to them, she was wiping the hard floor.

"Ehhmm... hi Lin, did you happen to see Lily and Latrez walked around? By themselves? Or with someone?"

"Kellie, these animals cannot really ran away by themselves though! Yet they were not bad at us?!"Gaya said.

"Sorry, well did you see someone walked with them?"

Linde leaned on her broom, "nope unless ehh no. I'll just ask my mother or my sister," she shrugged and walked to her sister, "Amber, have you seem Gaya and Kellie's horses, Latrez and Lily?"

"No, maybe mom has seen them. Mom! Did you happen to see Gaya and Kellie's horses?" screamed Linde.

"No, are they lost? Gee, much strength!" Said the mother.

Linde shrugged. "Sorry, have not seen them. I'll go back to sweeping. Bye."

"We are not giving up," sighed Gaya and made a fist of her hand. Kellie and Gaya walked on and arrived at Bass' home.

"Ehh... Bass, hi, have you seen our horses?"

"No, you mean that white horse Lily and dark brown Latrez? No."

"Okay, go back to throwing apples in that cart, or whatever you were doing. Bye," said Bas Kellie and Gaya waved off.

They passed a tiny house. "John lives there. John! Hey! Hello! Have you seen our horses? Latrez and Lily?"

A small boy came out of the narrow door. "Hey! Everything okay? "John asked.

"Well, no, not really," said Kellie "We're looking for Latrez and Lily."

"That's not so good, you're already gone to Jessy?" John asked.
"No." Kellie shrugged.

"You must go to her, you know how it is. She climbs every day for 5 hours in all road signs and lamp posts, and if she is above the post, she can see the whole city, so Jessy must know where it is! I would not know otherwise. Pardon me."

"Okay, thanks," said Gaya.

They trudged on. "I'm tired," sighed Kellie.

"We are going to Jessy, then I give up," said Gaya, "are you?"

Kellie nodded, "I, too, but then we just report it to the police, don't you think?"

She knocked on a large door. A lady opened it, Jessy's mother. "Jessy, May we talk to you?" Kellie asked.

"Jessy! Come in! Gaya and Kellie's here for you. Oh, sorry, girls, she is at the Appeldoorn Street, probably in a pile on the climb. She'll be home in an hour. You can also go to her."

"We do that, Madam, thank you." Kellie Gaya and waved goodbye to Jessy's mother and went to the Appeldoorn Street.

"How do we know where Jessy is? There are 20 million street lights," Kellie said.

"There," Gaya pointed to a high lamppost.

"Jessy! Down here!" Cried Kellie. Jessy looked down.

"Hey! I come down." She slid down the big pole and went they are, "what are you doing here?"

"We lost our horses," said Kellie, Gaya nudged Kellie's arm.

"What?! Oh, sorry, they're stolen," Kelly said. Gaya nodded.

"Really? Lily and Latrez? So pathetic!" Jessy said.

"And we wanted to ask if you may have seen them, because you always climb poles? And then you still see the whole city, at least, said John," Gaya said.

"He's smart, Indeed, I see the whole city, especially in this post," Jessy said proudly.

"Well? Have you seen them?" Asked Kellie and did an abrupt step forward.

"How do they look again?"

"A white and dark brown horse?" Gaya asked curiously.

"Nope, there are so many of those horses."
"Really, not two," cried Kellie offended.

"Sorry, but horse detection is not my thing," Jessy said.

"Well, thanks for your help," murmured Kellie and trudged on.

"Even as bad as this," said Gaya muttering as she pulled her foot from a thick gunk dirt.

"Exactly, you got in horse shit?"

"Think so," muttered Gaya.

"But that's fantastic!" exclaimed Kellie.

"Fantastic! Fantastic? Are you crazy?" Gaya shook her foot back and forth and the gunk flew around.

"Yup! We know the poop of our horses, right? We can smell it and then we will know whether they have been here!"

"Kellie, that's a very nice scent," said Gaya as she waved her hand to her nose "but what will we gain if we know they were here?"

"Think, dummy, then we can ask around or know that they might have been here along," Kellie said.

"Good, great idea," muttered Gaya.

"Never mind, I do it all myself!" Kellie said angrily.

"Where are you going?" cried Gaya.

"Blehhh, bleeh, blehhh, you're so ungrateful."

"What am I, the poop expert, be grateful?" asked Gaya.

"I healed your horse, or he won't be alive. You saw Latrez okay for a few kilometers and wanted to run?"

"Oh, just stop, he was not so ill," muttered Gaya.

"Yes, oh, I still love you so don't," grumbled Kellie, "Well, we go to the north." They walked together to the north and arrived at an old farm.

"Hi folks, what brings you here on this dirty day?" asked the farmer.

"We have lost our horses, and we are looking around asking if anyone has seen them, or so," Kellie said.
"Oh, oh, that's not good, no, no. Come here inside, then you can tell everything and you see, I'm also tired, come in," repeated the friendly farmer. They sat down on mini stools.

"Mom, Dad, who are they?" asked a few children.

"Stray people, I believe," said a wise young boy with glasses on.

"No, they are looking for something, maybe," said one girl.

"Good Laicha, they are looking for, you know what they are looking for?" asked the farmer. The farmer's wife looked cute, she was still young and had short black hair.

"No," said the children.

"Their horses. Have any of you seen them?" asked the farmer.

"What do they look like?" asked Ahammed.

"A white and a dark brown," said Gaya.

"No, no not seen," Ahammed said.

"I don't know, there are still so many of them." Said Kichala.

The old farmer looked at the little boy, "Kairan, did you?" asked the farmer. Kairan shook his head "no."

"Wait, Laicha....?" The woman looked at the little girl with the black hair. She looked a little scared when the father came in.

"What is going on here? Hey! Who are they?" said the farmer.

"What are your names actually girls?" asked the woman softly.

"I'm Gaya," said Gaya and pointed to Kellie "That's Kellie."

"Ah, okay," said the woman.

"It's Gaya and Kellie, they are looking for their horses, one white and one brown. Koron, have you seen them?" asked the farmer.

The farmer thought. "But wait!" He said suddenly, "they are together? Maybe kidnapped? Or taken? By a person in black, yes I have seen, there were seven men."

"Yes, they're together and someone in black. Wait!" Cried Kellie, "when I jumped out of bed because heard rustle and pounding horse's feet, I looked. I'm sure I saw a black figure standing my horse and pulling Lily!"

"Ah!" Said the farmer.
"Laicha, you now also have seen something?"

Laicha nodded and finally started talking. "I've seen them and they even talked to me. They said, 'don't tell anyone or else!" Laicha pointed to her neck, making a plain of her hand and let it slide down her neck.

"Boom!" cried Laicha and dropped to the ground with a bang. She sat back upright, "and the seven men were like shepherds or something, maybe cowboys or yes, they actually can be anything; researchers, who cut open animals," cried Laicha and fell backwards.

"Fine," muttered Kellie, "thank you Laicha. Sir, where did you see them exactly? Wait, can I just get a drawing pad?"

Gaya signaled Kellie and began to draw a man and then she tore the paper into a thousand shreds.

Gaya whispered softly, "she always does that when she is angry and stressed."

"1, 2, 3... well, where were we?" asked Kellie.

Kairan raised his hand, "ehh... people, shouldn't we start with the annual trek?"

The farmer's wife stood up, "that's right! Kellie, Gaya, uh... we will shortly do our trek, which we do every year, we will run a huge piece. I'm Lola, my husband is Koron, but I think you really need to go, sorry. Goodbye and good luck!"

"Wait," said Kellie "What should we do? Where did you see the guys again?"

"At the beach," Koron said.

"Good, but how we should go there? We are in the city, it is miles away, and where did they go?"

"*In Valariru*!" cried Laicha and stuck her finger in the air.

"Vale... what? Oh no? What is it and where is it? "Kellie asked incredulously.

"No, at least not that island, Valariru. You don't go there or you're dead. That place is full of scary creatures, no people!" Gaya said anxiously.

"Dead?" asked Kellie shocked "stone dead you mean!" she screamed. After recovering from the initial shock, Gaya and Kellie prepared for the big trip.

"You can go to that store, over there," said Lola, pointing through the window to a small black and white hut. "You can hire camels, which you will need on your journey."

"Thank you Lola," Kellie said.

"Camels Park is hot, you can rent or buy camels," said Koron "for an affordable price. The guy who works there is our best buddy, John, or Johnny, we always call him Johnny's Camels Parakeet."

"Thank you Koron," said Gaya.

"We will do our best," squeaked Kellie.

"For the horses you mean?" asked Gaya.

"Yes, and to stay alive," Kellie squeaked again.

"Oh, that stuff, well, we are not the best in handball, softball. We only excel in football. Come on dude, it's not that bad, we find our horses, "said Gaya, still not completely confident.

"Suddenly I miss Lily. I'm very sorry," sobbed Kellie and burst into tears.

"Quiet Kel," Gaya hit Kellie's arm, "Nothing happened. You cry when you lose something!"

Kellie looked at Gaya sadly

.

"What?" Gaya asked Ahammed who looked at her as if she had committed a crime. "What is wrong with keeping an unwise short sermon?"

"Sorry," Gaya said finally, "but we will go on the road. I miss Latrez too much and I'm scared."

Gaya swept the droplets under her eyes, Ahammed sorry, sorry Kel."

"Never mind," Kellie said with tears in her eyes.

"Thank you all for the help," Gaya nodded and pulled her backpack again a little tighter on her back.

"You're welcome girls, I hope you find them, and gently huh?" said Lola.

"Don't die eh!" Laicha shouted after, while she put her laces tight.

"Shall we try," Kellie nodded as if it were the most normal thing in the world.

Kellie and Gaya walked out of the little house and went to the hut. It was painted in zebra colors and in big red letters a sign hung on a chain "CAMELS PARK."

The 'p' hung sideways on a chain and now looked like "CAMELS ARK." Ding Dong. Kellie Gaya and walked into the store. In the corner was a small fat man with freckles, bristling red hair and glasses. He looked really laughable. He was even fatter than the thickest turd who lay on the ground at Kellie's feet.

"Hello, we'll hire camels," Gaya said with her nose completely squeezed, he had become completely red, pinching her nose so hard.
Kellie had tears in her eyes because she could only breathe through her mouth and that was not quite good.

"Who recommended you? How did you get here? "Replied the little, a little scary as a crow male.

"Lola and Koron who live near here. They said we could hire camels here," Kellie said with a red but also a bit purple face.

"Oh, lovely, nice people you are not? Especially Koron," laughed the male hoarsely.

"Yes, but we should borrow a camel?" Kellie talked it over uninterested.

"Borrow?" Snorted the man contemptuously.

"Yes," said Kellie like they could fall down in exactly 30 seconds.

"You're at the right place," laughed the male.

Camel ride

"Ehh... yes," said Gaya confidently, "we knew why we come to you."

"Choose only one. Rent costs 20 euros a camel. Bring them back after a month!"

"Yes," nodded Kellie "which is easy to ride?

"Chicho and Hessel, there." The man pointed to two little camels.

"Oh," said Kellie "thank you." They paid for the camels and took Chicho and Hessel.

"Well, how do you control such a beast?" Kellie asked.

"Oh lovely, open air!" She sniffed the delicious smell of the wind, but then grabbed her nose again.

Gaya watched in horror down to Chicho, who had dropped a large flan on the ground. "Getting out excited this thing."

Kellie jump on the camel and rode at full speed away.

"Wait for me," Gaya said with a purple face, and waddled behind her friend.

"Fine," said Kellie with a smile on her face, "we go to the beach with Chicho and Hessel."

"Ehh... Kel," Gaya looked petrified as to where Kellie was going.

"What?" Kellie asked as she alighted.

Gaya also stepped down, "Oh shit, behind you."

She looked behind her and saw two black men, and later a thick man wrapped in white with two horses, Latrez and Lily!

"Give back our horses!" Kellie stepped forward with her clenched fist, "or I'll beat that stupid face in the sand!" She shouted angrily.

"Kel, quiet!" Muttered Gaya. She was scared.

The man aimed his gun at Kellie and was about to shoot when the man in the white suit said, "Stop!"

The man dropped his gun down and looked at his boss as if he was crazy, "but boss..."

"Hush," snapped the man in white to the other man.

"Who are you?!" he asked sternly.

"Those who go down strike your people," said Kellie.

"Kel, quiet! Not so aggressive! Err... we are the bosses of the horses," Gaya said anxiously.

"Gaya, you recognize this gentleman? He was the bus driver!" Kellie said with contempt and with raised nose.

First Valariru characters

"What?" Gaya cried just a little too hard.

"Well?" Shrilled the white man "who are you?"

"That's what I like," sighed Gaya as if she had been told 100 times.

"That says nothing," cried the man and pulled the gun from his friend Hylo again from his pocket.

He pointed the gun at the girls and said something calmer now, "Well? What are your names?"

"Excites you huh?" Kellie bit the man, and Chico suddenly jumped and drove off like a rocket. Gaya rushed after her in Hessel.

"Come here," cried the white man. "That's an order, otherwise something happens with your horses!"

Abruptly she stood silent. Kellie drove staggering back. She still could not just leave their horses?

"I'm Kellie, that's Gaya," she said, "can we now have our horses back, we have to go!" She tried.
"Ke-le-that!" Hissed Gaya pissed. "What?" Kellie said with a wry smile.

"Okay, come with me, then you get your horses," said the white man.

"I'm Serge."

"What is your profession?" asked Kellie cunningly.

"It's none of your business!" cried Serge.

Kellie galloped a little ahead suddenly and blocked Serge's way and his men. She had a plan. She wanted to distract the men.

"Who is Laicha?" Kellie squeezed her eyes.

"Laicha? Ehh... I don't know who he is, "cried Serge, four chins went with his head as he shook violently back and forth from "No."

"Did you not forced to silence her?" Asked Kellie. Gaya understood her effort and meanwhile secretly pulled the straps of Lily and Latrez from the pockets of Hylo, who was not paying attention and was just sat smoking a cigarette.

Then she said quickly: "It's late we must go!" She galloped away quickly and the horses with him. Kellie gestured to a boat that was in the distance.

"Come here!" Serge shouted, then muttered something against Hylo, who aimed his gun and tried to shoot. Don't miss! Gaya and Kellie jumped from the camels, and ran with the horses and camels to the big boat. They both jumped into the boat and Gaya shouted, "Turn on that engine, I'm already rowing!" Fortunately, the engine started immediately and they spurt away in the middle of the sea.

"Lily," Kellie hugged her horse and Gaya too. The camels seemed to smile.

"Because of these little camels we have our horses back." Kellie hugged Chicho and Hessel around their necks and they carry on with the boat.

"What is actually on the boat there?" Gaya asked as she looked at the side of the boat.

"The Merfitchy, beautiful name," nodded Gaya and sat down right. "Euhhhh... where are we?" Kellie asked, a little anxious and looked around.

It was very foggy. They cannot see anything. The waves lapped against the edge of the Merfitchy.

"Are we acquitted somewhere?" muttered Gaya.

They went a little further through the fog. The boat bobbed up and down. "Ehh... where are we? Not on the normal sea, "murmured Kellie. The water in the sea turned pale greenish purple.

"This is really crazy water," said Gaya, she put her finger in the sea, and then put her finger in her mouth, "lemonade and pepper," she said surprised.

"The lemonade is still nice but it also tasted like pepper!" Kellie grimaced when also tasted the strange sea.

"This is not normal!" Gaya looked at a large chest that had been lying all the way on the boat, "what is this? We have been so busy with flights in a boat that we don't even know what that is, and who is this boat anyway?"

Kellie grabbed the strange coffin and tore the lid.

"Don't open it!" She screamed. "Give me here," Gaya grabbed the thing off Kellie and looked at it carefully.

"Interesting," she murmured, looking around wildly. She saw an iron rod in the water. She took it out of the water, shook it back and forth to get it soggy and then pushed off the bottom piece below the lid.

"Pull!" She called to Kellie. Together they pulled as hard as possible. The thing flew open and she looked wide-eyed at what it contained: cans of cola and other drinks, sandwiches, jam jars, pasta, peanut butter, slices of cheese, a jar of pickles, a bag of sweets, large marshmallows, lots of candy and much more. It was like a magic box. There was so much in it.

Kellie grabbed a small square box and ripped the top off it with all his might. "Choco balls," she cried as if they had arrived in the land of plenty, and then pop a large choco ball in her mouth.

Gaya grabbed a jar with English drops and then saw a can opener lying in the coffin. She grabbed it and opened it. She popped a blue English licorice in her mouth and chewed on it. "Great," she muttered.

Meanwhile, Kellie finished her choco ball and looked at the box carefully at what else was in it. There was also a pocketknife. Then she picked up a cheese sandwich, which was tightly wrapped in a plastic bag of sturdy plastic. Gaya snatched it from Kellie's hands and cut it open with the penknife. She immediately put the sandwich in her mouth. Kellie growled.

Suddenly Lilly's huge head sniffed inside the coffin inside and instantly snatched a sandwich from the chest without noting that there was plastic around. Kellie grabbed the penknife from Gaya's hands and opened the sandwich bag. She pulled a sausage and sliced it in half and gave one each to Lily and Latrez. Gaya grabbed a can and opened it and she drank greedily. Kellie did the same.

The boat with all animals

Meanwhile Chicho and Hessel fight over a syrup. Kellie squeezed her fine tin and threw it back in the chest, Gaya grabbed a jar of pickles and greedily ate it.

Suddenly, Kellie saw a thing wrapped in foil paper. She grabbed it and tore the sheet of paper there. She saw a rolled pancake in it. She licked her lips and turned her back to Gaya secretly. Gaya noticed nothing, who was greedily cramming one pickle in her mouth. Kellie grabbed a knife that was in the chest and opened the chocolate paste. They also picked up the can opener and opened the pasta. She stuck the knife into the paste and smeared it on her pancake. It was difficult without a board. Kellie sometimes smeared it wrong and thereby touched her pants and her shirt. That did not matter her.

When the pancake was finally finished, she wanted it in her mouth. Suddenly she heard a gull above her head so hard that she screamed and jumped from the shock. The pancaked dropped from her hands and fell with a loud splash in the water. Kellie sighed and looked after the pancake he dipped up and down like a sponge. What a misfortune! Suddenly she saw a shark emerge and grabbed the pancake and swallowed it.

"Gaya" cried Kellie shocked, "a shark, there, meters away from us!"

"What is it?" asked Gaya, who was very interested in sharks.

"A little whitish. He is quite large and has huge jaws!" screamed Kellie. "He can prey on every live creature!" She pressed her hands to her cheeks until they were as red as the red tip of a match.

"Ah, interesting, that is a very rare shark, ehh... ehh.... Shark?... Engine!" Gaya screamed.

"An engine?" asked Kellie still with red cheeks.

"No, get out quickly, it's a great white shark! Or the man shark!"

"Is he human, then?" asked little Kellie shambling with wide eyes.

"No! This is the only shark that eats people."

"What? Well also other things apparently," noted Kellie annoyed," because that stupid shark has just ate my pancake!" screamed Kellie lustily. The engine was not working.

"Oh, no shit out of fuel!"

They rowed as fast as they could, but the shark caught up with them, he grabbed the oar and Kellie pulled was into the water.

"Kellie!" screamed Gaya, her eyes were wet and she saw nothing. Latrez accidentally pushed Gaya with her big ass into the water. Gaya fell forward into the water. In the distance she saw a red trickle. She was afraid that Kellie was seized by the shark, but at the same time, swam away for her life. Kellie had a big gash over her calf.

Gaya quickly climbed back into the boat and pulled her girlfriend with all his might in the boat. Kellie fell sideways on the boat, but the shark was still there. It jumped to the top! He grabbed Kellie's long hair, who was hurled overboard and was nearly pulled back into the water, but the only thing he caught was a tiny bit her hair. The shark swam away.

Kellie was not red in her cheeks, but her calf was red with blood. "You okay, Kel?" Gaya asked shocked.

Kellie nodded, "a little."

Gaya rummaged quickly in the coffin and saw that in the corner was an old box. She closed the coffin and walked carefully to the edge of the boat. She grabbed the box and ran back to her old place.

"Give it," Kellie grabbed the box from Gaya's hands and examined it carefully.

"Ouch! It really hurts," she rubbed her sore calf, then looked at her hand, which was red with blood. "*FIRST AID FOR REAL EMERGENCY OR SERIOUS* EMERGENCY," Kellie read the box. Gaya took the box back from Kellie and carefully opened the lid.

"Oops," so the lid popped off the box.

"Well, this thing has had its best time," grumbled Kellie. Gaya took out a box of bandages and pulled out the box of 19 patches. "This should be enough to cover your entire calf." Gaya said, and took it out of the box.

"That does not make sense," said Kellie, "there are 20 patches. In such a case, maybe you will need 1 or 2, then." Kellie took a larger patch.

"No, I already have something," said Gaya. She stuffed the 19 patches back in the box and grabbed another carton.

"What have you got in there? You better use the large patch that I just suggested."

"No, look," Gaya took the pocketknife out of the crate and cut the box open. There was a whole roll of bandage. "So?" asked Kellie, "My calf does not hurt though!" Kellie dropped her hand back down her calf and showed it to Gaya. With an arrogant voice she said, "You see? No drop of blood."

"Ehh, Kel, have you played with a giant red paint sometime? Jesus, your whole hand was covered in blood." Kellie looked at her hand. Gaya was right, the wound was pretty and it was all red. Kellie grinned like a farmer with a toothache and put her hand into the sea. She left a trail of blood behind.

"Where is the shark, anyway?" Kellie asked suddenly.

"Ehh... don't know," said Gaya and looked terrified at the water. No shark in sight. Kellie looked back and saw a large sail boat with a fishing net it in the distance. There was a big beast in the net. Shark! The boat came closer and Kellie stood up, and waved violently with her arms.

"Over Here! Right Here! Here we are! Help! Here we are, with a few camels and... ouch!" Kellie rubbed her calf, "and two horses."

They came closer. But to their horror and terror, the drivers and crew were no people.

The boat and the girl

The men on board were small and dark and were either very thick or very thin. The captain had a mustache, and a long beard that reached his feet on the ground. He was small, had large black shoes, piercing eyes that pierced you and a penetrating stare. His kinky hair, narrow eyes, and his little hat that was not really fantastic on his head fitting all that frizzy hair pinned up, were terrifying but also crazy to see.

At the front of the boat printed in gold letters: "CEF VALARIRU, CHONAS." The captain was called Cef and the boat was called Chonas.

Then he suddenly pulled a little girl with him, that they apparently caught. She looked very frightened. The captain gave her a push forward. He wanted to throw her in the water, so they had to feed the shark, which he had caught in a net. The next moment he said something unintelligible and suddenly disappeared. The shark was free. The girl fell down the big boat with a scream, but was able to grab the bottom of a hanging rope.

"Row, Gaya" cried Kellie. Gaya rowed as hard as she could. Kellie stood on the edge of the boat and stretched her arms. They could get the girl and pulled her in their boat. She succeeded. The shark which again came to swim, took a leap and grabbed the girl's shoe. The shark got nothing so it swam away again angry and offended.

"Row, Gaya" Kellie called again. She placed her gently in the middle of the boat. Kellie grabbed an oar and began to row. The small Captain shouted: "Who are you?" He had a scary voice. He sounded like a crow with a toothache. Kellie wanted to shout, 'nothing to you' but Gaya shouted: " I'm Gaya and that is Kellie, well bye!"

"Give *Hessel* back!" said the little man. "We rented Hessel! We should not give it away!" cried Kellie and put her arms around the camel. "You don't know what Hessels mean, right" snapped the man. Oh, that's true, you don't know what that means in our language, stupid me. Hessels in your language is 'people'! So give that Hessel back that you girlfriend Kakkelie has just caught!"

"My name is Kellie" improved Kellie. "No Kakkelie or whatever you said. We give, chips back." Kellie hold back her leg.

"You want to get hurt? All the easier, grab them!" shouted the captain.

The girl suddenly grabbed a rope from the boat and a stone. She rolled the stone in the rope and made a thick knot. The girl was a Chinese girl, dark colored, with hair to her waist in a ponytail. She had black hair and was of small stature. She hurled the stone and the rope above her head and then threw it to the boat. The stone came with a bang on the head of a man. He fell down.

"Row" cried the girl. The three of them rowed. It went pretty fast.

"Wait," said the girl, she took a small device from her pocket and pressed a button. There was a huge whooshing sound. She turned the thing on the water and they shot forward. They were gone so fast that the boat of the strange men had disappeared from sight.

"Cool trick," nodded Kellie, "what's your name anyway?"

"Vaela," said the girl.

"I'm Kellie and this is Gaya. How do you get those gadgets?" Kellie asked curiously.

"My father was an inventor. I also have this." She took a small device in the form of a leaf (of a tree) and handed it to Kellie.

"Great. I see. Why there is no link around it?" asked Vaela.

"Don't know," laughed Kellie, and she bandaged it around anyway

"Stop, let that piece open," Vaela said. Kellie turned back a bit and said, "That's the wound."

The wound had stopped bleeding so you could see the size of the wound.

"Click on the stalk of the leaf and hold it gently against the wound," Vaela told Kellie. Kellie pressed and held it over her wound. The wound turned yellow, and Kellie shouted: "Awww! That hurts!"

"But I assure you, it cures everything," nodded Vaela. Kellie looked at the wound and took the bandage off.

"I feel nothing!" Suddenly, the wound began to give a light and all the colors of the rainbow radiated. Kellie looked admiringly at her wound. Her whole calf was healed! It was like a miracle.

"Do you know where you are?" asked Vaela worried.

"At sea?" Kellie wanted to be funny. "I mean really, a disturbed sea?"

"Well, you have not even noticed where in the sea you are?!" exclaimed Vaela startled.

"No, why is that so crazy? We really don't know the world. But a purple sea that tastes too weird, I never have actually seen. We sometimes sit on the Big Purple Sea?" said Kellie.

"Another mistake, come on! You really don't know?" She put her hands on her hips.

"What? What? Say where we are! Please," said Gaya.

"Sure I'm going to tell you," nodded Vaela.

"We are on the *Sweet Seas Valariru*," she said in a whisper.

"What?!" shouted Kellie.

The seagulls were flying and screeching on the bent flag of Merfitchy.

"Where is it then, and what are we doing here?" Kellie asked incredulously.

"Kellie, you wanted to risk your life anyway for the horses? Well, now we have them, and we are here. Would it really be so bad that we are here?" Gaya asked, while she stuffed six English licorice in her mouth.

"Yes, but now it's for nothing," muttered Kellie. She grabbed a big chocolate bar from the chest that she stuffed in her mouth greedily. Then she gave Vaela a piece of chicken in front of her.

"Share?" Kellie asked munching.

"No, I'm a vegetarian," said Vaela, and held her hands to her mouth and shook his head.

"Vegetarian? I did not expect that of you," said Gaya still munching like crazy. She swallowed the English drop and threw back a cracker in her mouth, followed by a chocolate.

"Chocolate?" Kellie asked Vaela. She shook her head no. "Huh? You don't wanna eat? That explains why you're so slim."

That was true. Vaela was very slim and looked healthy, despite her length and width. She had a cheerful face and small eyes glistening friendly, even though they were such slits.

"I'm allergic to chocolate, but I think it's very nice," she said.

"Oh, that's too bad for you, I am allergic to some types of medications," said Kellie.

"I'm allergic to rugs and dust," said Gaya.

"Don't you feel a little acidic?" asked Kellie.

"No, I hate when my palate gets so weird and annoying," Vaela said.

"You don't meant that. How about brown bread with seeds in it and cheese on it?" Kellie rattled on. She reached out for a plastic bag.

"I'm not so fond of burgers," Kellie stuck her tongue out and stuck her finger in.

"Good," said Vaela, "I like it. Bread is nice and soft."

"You like brown bread? With seeds?" asked Kellie. Vaela nodded.

"Sometimes, I also like raw fish!"

"Oh," said Gaya, "special taste you have."

Kellie fumbled in the wonder-box, which is not empty but seemed to touch and pulled out the pocketknife.

"Here." Vaela cut the bag opened with a penknife and threw it back into the box.
"Why are you here?" Vaela asked with his mouth full.

"Well, our horses were stolen and we visited almost the entire village to ask if anyone has seen them. We came upon an old farmhouse, and asked around there. A girl, named Laicha, said she had seen what and when told us that the thieves wanted to go to Valariru. They might actually say anything, but thanks to her we knew it, so we also went. We encountered the crooks who stole our horse on the beach. They wanted to shoot at us, that's why we had to run, so we jumped on this boat and sailed away. What a story, eh?"

"Laicha?!" Vaela stood with a jerk. The camels and horses behind her fell back in terror. "You mean Laicha Kirono from Lasseon?"

"Well I don't know what her name is," Kellie shrugged.

"Little light brown girl? Dark black hair? Big eyes? Thick hair? Dark pink violet eyes?" asked Vaela.

"Yes, yes, yes, yes and yes!"

"Her father's name is Koron? Her mother is Lola? And she has six brothers and sisters?"

"Yup! Do you mean the same Laicha" cried Kellie.

"She is my best friend!" carried Vaela happily.

"Well, it goes well with her, they have now started to pull the loop," said Gaya

. "Yup? Oh yes, she had once told about it," Vaela said.

"Yes!" exclaimed Kellie happily.

"What are you so happy about?" Gaya asked Kellie and looked at her.

"No! But look over there!" Kellie pointed with outstretched arm to a large piece of land.

"Land!" exclaimed Kellie.

"Land? Where?" asked Vaela. Gaya held her hand over her eyes against the bright sun to see the island.

"Row" Vaela said. They rowed all together to the island, it seemed quite large. Kellie was so excited that she lay the oars down neatly in place. "Awww Kellie, chill!" Gaya said a little angry. But Kellie already ran to the beach.

The fall of Vaela and Kellie

"What a cool little village, is it not?" Kellie looked around excitedly. Vaela could tell that they arrived on the island called Valariru, also called Death Island.

"Kellie, please be quiet," Gaya snapped at Kellie.

"Don't be so cranky," laughed Kellie.

"Why do you laugh? We are in the island of Death!" Gaya said panicky.

"Wait a minute," murmured Vaela, and ran into a lady who picked apples.

"Madam, may I ask you something?" Vaela held out her hand, and something very strange happened. Her hand went right through the body of the woman. Suddenly all people disappeared and the entire village was wiped out. It was suddenly an empty plain!

"Nice, it seemed like Mars though?" Gaya asked at startled Kellie.

"Mars? Oh no, this is..."

"Shhh," Vaela interrupted Kellie.

"Hush," Vaela said again, "I hear something." The girls stood anxiously behind a piece of stone that lay below.

"Who is that?" Kellie suddenly asked, pointing to a large greenish ball on the ground.

"Who is that? What is that? "Gaya improved her friend.

"I'm going to see," said Vaela confidently.

She walked up to the big green thing. Now it was *so* quiet that it seemed like it was just a ball, but it was not. Once Vaela stretched her arm out to pick the thing, it slobbered away such that you will see a huge green ball with a girl in it.

"Ewwww," Kellie ran on the thing.

"Stop!" Gaya screamed at Kellie and grabbed her arm.

"That thing swallows you up. That pudding is dangerous!" Gaya screamed anxiously.

"What should we do?" screamed Kellie. Suddenly she saw a box on the ground. Vaela, who was in the pudding, waved and shouted.

"There are my devices from my father! Use them! Cut the electrical pocketknife and open the pudding!"

Kellie grabbed the box. "But what if this thing gobbles you up?" Kellie asked Vaela.

She nodded yes, "then I cut it open," she said.

"Okay."

Kellie grabbed the box and pulled out a small device. Vaela shook her head 'no'. Kellie grabbed a few devices, but Vaela kept shaking her head. Kellie came with a red square device. Vaela finally nodded 'yes'. Kellie threw the device to the green pudding and he gobbled it up. Vaela stretched her arm with difficulty and grabbed the device at her feet. It was hard to move around in the pudding, too, that 'no' and 'yes' shake was difficult.

She finally got hold of the device and cut it open. The pudding seemed to be water and slob when it went apart. You heard a squelching sound, like the pancake Kellie dropped in the sea. She tapped her finger against her forehead. Vaela fell heavily to the ground. Her hair was covered in green goo. But even that faded. Kellie ran to Vaela.

"Fortunately, there is nothing," she sighed. "Yes, I was frightened to death when he slobbered on me."

"I understand," Gaya laughed, but she laughed like a farmer with toothache.

"Let's go," Kellie said and watched the Merfitchy boat slipped away. Then she saw a plastic bag on the ground, and there were marshmallows in. "Look! Marshmallows!" Kellie's face lit into a smile.

"Kel, quiet. We cannot trust anything here!" Gaya said, and glanced around.

"We can at least look?" Said Kellie and ran to the scene. "Don't know," said Vaela, "we can better rely on what Gaya said."

"Why?" Kellie protested and grabbed the plastic bag with marshmallows.

"Cat's head," Gaya hissed. Kellie could not resist and put a marshmallow in her mouth. Suddenly she widened her mouth wide and let the marshmallow fall out of her mouth; "Yuck!" Kellie violently grabbed her tongue and began to scratch hard.

"What? What is the problem now?" Vaela asked.

"It..." Kellie could not finish her sentence, the ground began to shake and rumbled under her and the ground made holes by the quake. Kellie fell down into a deep hole with a shock. Gaya and Vaela were afraid to watch, but Kellie was totally gone.

Gaya's misfortune

"Kel" cried Gaya and looked anxiously at the black depths. She did an abrupt step forward.

"Wait," Vaela said. She clicked on a heavy brown device in her hands, a little helicopter came out and at the bottom was a handle. Vaela tied it around her hand and said confidently to Gaya, "If I don't come back, look in the box." Vaela put the box down.

"Everything works on a button, anywhere is a button when you press it, and you automatically know what to do. Wish me strength."
Vaela jump into the deep hole, and disappeared.

"Strength," Gaya said dramatically. "I will do what I have to do, like Superman." Gaya said, clenching her fist. Then she looked back anxiously. It was an empty plain. She chirped, "I'm also fallen, or whatever you call it." She looked anxiously and then looked back with a frightened face in the deep hole. "What the hell am I supposed to do?" she thought.

Five minutes later...

"Poor me, Vaela and Kel did not come back!" She said in a dramatic tone like five minutes before.

"Hello?" Gaya looked suddenly afraid. "I'm coming!" She cried to the hole under her. Because when she looked behind her, the bus driver was standing there.

Gaya looked anxiously around and grabbed a stick lying nearby. She threw the stick to the bus driver, but dodged it with his thick body. Gaya jumped aside as he threw back the stick. He pointed behind him. There stood Latrez and Lily, Hessel and Chicho. They were attached to an iron chain.

"Release them!" cried Gaya and clenched her fist.

"Why, so I have a bone to pick with you, "he grinned.

"Sorry, I'm not an apple," chuckled Gaya, "that you cannot peel. Let everyone free otherwise I'll peel you!" She tried.

"Me? Me? Haha, you make me laugh," he laughed with a hoarse voice.

"Serge," Gaya murmured.

"You cannot peel me." He shook his head no, and his four chins went along. "We peel you!" Behind the bus driver, six men appeared. Corro, Dich Esso, Vanga, Milaar, Hylo and Caoa.

"Ehhh... no thanks, I don't like apples," Gaya laughed like a farmer with toothache.

"Then that's bad luck!" exclaimed Corro and hit his pocket knife open. Gaya quickly grabbed Vaela's box.

"That box looks familiar to me," muttered Serge, the bus driver. "Did you see that annoying girl? Vaela or something?"

"Vaela," Gaya corrected Serge.

"I knew it! I had surrendered her to Cef! He's one of my best. How did they come to you? That bitch?"

"She's not a bitch, she's a wise girl, but in a nice primitive way," said Gaya pissed.
"Fascinating," he screamed. "Apple turnovers attacks!" He shouted to his men. They came screaming with swords and pistols towards her. Gaya fumbled nervously with the box and pulled out a box from the size of a large ant.

"I still have nothing?" Murmured Gaya anxiously, but pressed the button, which was as large as the leg of an ant. It so happened at the same

with Vaela. The pudding came out and joined everyone including Gaya. However, she's some kind protected as she hung at the top.

Gaya in the blue pudding

The men fired at the pudding, but the bullets and knives just bounced back! Gaya laughed. A helping pudding!

"I can't peel you? Amehoela, then I am the queen of Asia!" Gaya grinned. The advantage of this pudding was that you could have those moving well.

Gaya then suddenly saw Kellie and Vaela appeared. They were saved! Gaya sighed with relief, but when she saw that the men she froze her face. Vaela muttered something under her breath, which was not understood, and suddenly the three were them were in the pudding! This pudding was indeed blue. The previous bad was green. Vaela sat at the top of the pudding, upside down, so her head sat with Kellie's leg on the floor of the pudding.

Vaela saw her box suspended in the pudding, she stretched out her arm and grabbed her chest. She saw a green key sitting in the box. "*The Maka*, yes!" Vaela took the green key, with which the square that was hanging on the chain and the chain itself was green, everything. She pressed a button.

Kellie stared at the ground, namely the pudding broke away from the ground! They flew into the sky. Vaela muttered something under her breath and the next moment Chicho, Hessel, Latrez and Lily were also crammed in the large convex of the pudding!

"Lily! Finally!" Kellie walked through the pudding in slow motion to her horse, who was looking around dazed. "Hey" Vaela gave the box to Kellie.

"You have to keep the box with gadgets. It will still come in handy. Now I'm going to take the camels away, right to Jan's Camels Park okay?"
"Yeah okay, but you will go now? We don't know how all this works, and we're just good friends!" Gaya cried a little scared. Kellie sighed. She looked through the blue pudding. Serge and the men were still under it. The men tried everything to break the pudding, but nothing worked.

"Well I want Hessel and Chicho to be safe, just go," sighed Kellie.

"What? We'll be left to ourselves Kel?" screamed Gaya. She fell so far back that she almost fell out of the pudding. Because nothing could just walk in there.

"You will hear from us!" cried Gaya. But Vaela continued.
"This will ask you questions, so we can keep in touch," she nodded, gave a purple cube and ignored Gaya's remark. Kellie got a blue cube, Vaela himself took a pink cube. "This is the *Gichi*."

Suddenly Kellie and Gaya saw a glass come out of the block. Vaela saw Kellie and Kellie saw Vaela and Gaya. Gaya saw Kellie and Vaela and Vaela saw Gaya and Kellie.

"Gosh, your father made this?! Really cool," Kellie said. Vaela nodded.

"Then it's time to go." Vaela pulled something out of the box, a large triangular shiny thing, it was dark.

"This is a *JOOKI*, with this device you bring someone back to where the person belongs. You only need to say the name. Jan's Camel Park, Chicho, Hessel, NOW!"

Hessel and Chicho flew out the pudding and disappeared in the air, back to Jan's camel park.

Vaela day

"I'm okay now. I had promised my father that I would return, alive," Vaela said.

"Vaela's villa n..." But Vaela could not finish her sentence.

"Wait!" Kellie cried. "You said everything worked a button, but this was not a button, you just said it!"

"Some devices don't have a button, no," Vaela said.

"But how do we know what we have to say?" Kellie asked.

"Just say what you want and that happens. There are two devices where you have nothing to say, that's our *Gichi's*, the blocks which we can make and can see each contact."

Vaela grabbed her pink cube.

"Oh, that's, okay and what else?" Kellie asked.

"The *Jooki*. That was the thing." Vaela grabbed the large dark green triangular object.

"It lets you send someone so back to his place. Something like this: Serge, to the beach of Asia, NOW"!

Kellie and Gaya strained to look at the blue pudding back to the ground. Serge flew into the air and disappeared.

"Boss! Where are you? "Caoa looked anxiously at the sky. But Serge was gone.

"Ooh, magic them all away!" Cried Gaya. Vaela muttered a whole sentence, and yes, one by one the men disappeared.

"Wow great, gone are those creeps. Your father invents stuff. He must be famous, "Kellie said.

"No, but he is enriched with it," said Vaela, "We live in a big house."

"Villa? Man, you're really rich, "sighed Kellie. Gaya nodded, "I wish I were you."

"Oh yeah? Well is not that much fun though."

"Why not?" asked Gaya.

"Just," snapped Vaela suddenly.

"Oh, well sorry," blurted Gaya.

"What are you doing in Valariru?" Kellie looked at Vaela questioningly.

"My father was a professor, inventor. He was a treasure, but my mother was so mean. She wanted me to be an inventor. She said, "You can earn good money for us!" But I want to be a vet and she says that's bad for me, with all that blood and all. But that is not so, what is she referring to?" sighed Vaela.

Kellie grabbed a pad from her backpack and drew a face. Kellie worked diligently on it. She wrote:

Hi, you'll be terribly missed. You are so convenient, nice and smart. I miss you already. Why do you have to call off right now? You're just about to tell about yourself. Come again when we come home. Send a note. If you get no response, you already know something in happened in Valariru. My house number and street number is number 8. I will miss you. Greetings Kel.

Kellie tore the paper from her notebook and put the piece of paper and the notepad in her backpack.

"What did you do?" asked Vaela.

"Nothing," muttered Kellie.

"Now I'm going," Vaela said.

"But why are you here?" Gaya asked. Vaela hit her eyes.

"Sorry, but I have to go now." She picked up the *Jooki*.

"Vaela's villa, Vaela, now!" Vaela flew out of the pudding. She flew into the air and disappeared.

"No! Vaela!" exclaimed Kellie startled.

The Gichi

Strange creatures

"Where the hell should we go?" Gaya looked around. Kellie saw Lilly looked tired. She jumped on Lily and looked around.

"What is it?" asked Gaya.

"I'm looking for water. My water pad is empty when I let Latrez had a drink."

"That was ditch water," chuckled Gaya.

"So what?" snapped Kellie?

"Maybe there is some water," Gaya galloped a little further. There was a huge stone with a small pool of water.

"Here is something. I don't know if it is enough," said Gaya.

Kellie walked Lily on the leash to pee. She bent down and looked at the puddle.

"I'll try," she murmured and put her water pad in the water cushion pool. You could hear a little slurping. It stopped. Kellie watched her water cushion. "It's only a quarter full, I have not much."

"Kellie, Kellie! There, look." Gaya looked anxiously at Kellie. "Behind you!"

Kellie turned with a jerk. There was a huge beast. It had short hair and six eyes, looking at her slyly. It grunted hard and showed its great short-haired dog hurtling down, right along Kellie's ear. Kellie jumped happily aside. Her water pad fell to the ground and the claw of the beast pierced the cushion. The inflated balloon snapped with a bang. Kellie screamed in terror, for she saw the beast's hairy paw whiz down again. Kellie could just dodge, but slipped on the water from the pillow and cried out in fear. It again whizzed its claw right past Kellie.

Lily suddenly came into action. She took a run up and stood in front of her boss. The claw made a big scratch on Lily's back.

"Lily," Kellie screamed anxiously. The horse moaned and slumped on the ground. Kellie grabbed a piece of the collapsed water cushion, which was wet from the water. It was very cold. She put the piece of pad on the wound. The monster glared. It hit again with its claw. It whizzed down.

"That's enough!" snapped Kellie and grabbed the box, she threw it with a blow to the head of the monster. It fell backwards. Kellie reached into the box and picked up a large wooden device. It had holes on all sides. Kellie picked it up and clicked a silver button. There was a crazy big knife. Kellie threw it with all his might against the beast. The came right up next to the monster, but the plane scratched its body. Kellie lay panting on the ground.
"Where is Vaela's healing potion?" Kellie grabbed the box violently and the gadgets were flying. Kellie sighed and picked up the paper. She held it up Lily's wound, clicked on the stalk, and a blue and yellow drop fell on Lily's wound. The wound began to give light and all the colors of the rainbow radiated as with Kellie's wound. Lily stood up and waved her tail. Kellie smiled cheerfully.
"Nice, we succeeded. Now let's please continue."

But suddenly Gaya stood with a small long-haired beast. It had long black hair and brown over its eyes and feet. One can see three nails at the bottom of each leg.

"What is *that*?" asked Gaya with disgust and pointed to the thing. She pulled Latrez's belt and pranced. Gaya calmed Latrez. Kellie looked with wonder at the creature.

"It's pretty cool. Is it dangerous?" asked Kellie. It just stared at them but said: "*Eisoa Gidolla Valariru*. I'm *Chessova*." said the beast.

"You're Chessova? What a terrible name," chuckled Gaya.

"No Gaya, he *is* a Chessova," Kellie said.

"A kind of long-haired goblin?" Gaya burst out laughing. The little Chessova did not seem to like that Gaya laughed at him. He made his hands into a fists (It looked more like a ball of wool) and murmured whole crazy words. Suddenly the balls of wool were all red like fire. The Chessova cried "Fire Ball" and pointed it at Gaya. The fiery red ball came whooshing towards her, she screamed, but it did nothing. She fell with Latrez with a blow to the ground. She lay motionless. The Chessova had disappeared.

"Gaya, stand up. Hey, what is this?" Kellie picked up a shiny red oval device from Vaela's chest. It was decorated in gold letters and read "discovery." Kellie grabbed the red device and clicked on a silver button. A door opened and it looked like a mobile that you could unfold. There was a crib sheet, on which stood:

Type the name of the animal or thing that you're looking for, and you can read all this information about them. Vaela.

Kellie was shocked. How could Vaela possibly know that they need a mobile that they called Mobic? Kellie thought for a second longer and typed *Chessova'* in. There was a short story:

Chessova are nasty beasts. They are smart, intelligent and they throw a Fireball buggy at someone they don't like. They are also quick to anger and are easily offended. You should be careful not to go against such a beast. The Fireball can sometimes be deadly.

The story was not over but Kellie looked anxiously at Gaya who was still lying on the floor... She read on quickly:

But not always, because there are drugs that professors, scholars, inventors and physicians make. The drug is in a kind of box or container, and it always has the shape or appearance of a plant. Handy to know: When the Chessova uses the fireball on an individual, the individual then becomes unconscious for a long time. It ensures that he gets away quickly after the attack.

Kellie smiled, she knew the device. She grabbed the box and went to Gaya. She took the paper and held it up Gaya's mouth, clicked on the stem and a yellow blue drop reappeared.

Moments later Gaya shot to her feet. Kellie laughed. "I just read something about that Chessova! He is very easily offended, you should read it," Kellie kept the red phone for Gaya's nose, and Gaya read with a red head all information about the Chessova.

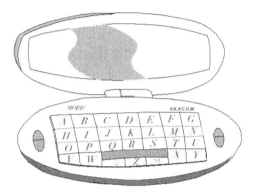

The Mobic

Waterfall

"Whaah, this is as boring as I don't know what," said Kellie and squeezed Lily's reins more firmly in her hand.

"Do you?" smiled Gaya, who had been restored by the fire attack of the Chessova, "I have other piles of candy in my bag."

"Candy?" Kellie gave a gentle tug on Lily's reins because she wanted to stop immediately.

"What you have now with that?" Kellie said if she was not interested.

"You're just jealous, but quiet dude. Because you're my best friend, you are allowed one piece of candy per 200 kilometers!" teased Gaya. Gaya brought a broad smile on her face.

"Oh give me a break," Kellie blurted out and rode at full gallop.

"Why are you frustrated!" teased Gaya.

"Where is that well again?" Kellie snapped back.

"You don't have a drawing pad? Can you just let yourself cool down by drawing and then tear it!" taunted Gaya. Kellie squeezed her eyes.

"Put briefly normal."

"Why So?"

"Therefore," chuckled Kellie.

Gaya raised her arrogant nose. "Phew, cocky," said Gaya snapped.

"Phew, cocky," Kellie imitated Gaya with a fussy voice, "nice mood did you say, Pooh, I'm lucky with such a girlfriend!" Kellie said.

Gaya pulled Latrez's reins tighter. "You'll strangle the beast," grumbled Kellie.

"No, I don't."

"Well."

"Don't be a fool."

"Well, dude!"

"Ah still love your head!"

"I?" Kellie wasn't able to finish her sentence because Latrez suddenly slowed down so hard that Gaya fell over and was left dangling on a stone.

"Latrez stop. Don't go down the abyss and the waterfall!" screamed Kellie.

Gaya still dangled on the stone. "Help me Kel, please," screamed Gaya anxiously, but it was too late, the rock broke off and Gaya fell down.

"Gayaaaaaaaaaaaaaa!" screamed Kellie. She had tears in her eyes and her hair dangling over the abyss.

Kellie gave herself a slap and then chased Gaya. The horses just stood there. But the horses also thought for a second and chased their owners. They went down all together. They fell with a loud bang in the water. Fortunately the water was very deep. They were swept away by the current and came to a lake that lay among all the trees. They drove to the side and the horses scrambled painfully to the side. Kellie looked beside her, with a tired and anxious face. There laid Gaya, but she said nothing and had her eyes closed. Was she dead?

Kellie scrambled to her feet slowly. She looked at Gaya, who still lay looking drowned, but she breathed. Kellie watched the lake with big, wet eyes. Then she looked with even bigger eyes upward, at the giant waterfall. She did not know how high they had fallen, perhaps a kilometer or more?

Suddenly she saw a bright red piece of paper floating in the water. "What a pollution, surely one of those *Munka's*, which are the only almost-humans on this island. I think I will not find any Valariru people on this crazy island!"

Kellie walked to the lake and pulled the paper out. It was a crib sheet. There was something written on it:

"Good Kel, nicely done, you risked *your life for Gaya. That's very brave of you. I myself had not dared, well, keep it up, Vaela.*"

Kellie's hands began to tremble. Vaela knew everything. How could she suddenly throw papers everywhere so that Kellie will see it?

"Gaya?" Kellie looked back at Gaya, who was still unconscious.

"Are you dead?" asked Kellie. Gaya still did not answer. Kellie looked at the piece of paper. No, that is not possible. The paper is blank again!

Hotel Larmana Valariru

Fortunately Gaya was a little dazed from the fall. She had a bruised ankle, a large wound on her right leg that had been cured with the wonder gadget and a lot of scratches everywhere, Further they had a lot of pain everywhere. After a long rest they went again.

Kellie and Gaya arrived in a strange town. There were several creatures, but no people. *Halloja's Chessova's Googels, Magare, Uluzen, Vatty's Munka's* - who were not too friendly to Gaya and Kellie - and *Ossoozen*.

"Ehh... sorry, do you know an inn or something for us?" asked Gaya to *Uluz* who was passing, but he walked by muttering. "Gosh, we seemed to have Joseph and Mary here today. Looking for a hostel or a room!" Cried Kellie.

"So what! We're looking for a room?" Gaya moaned after the pains.

"Ehh... sorry," Kellie tapped the back of a Chessova, "do you have a room for us?"

"Ehh...?" cried the Chessova.

'No, we have much," muttered Kellie. The Chessova put his fists together, was a little upset by Kellie's reaction. Just before he wanted to do something, Kellie and Gaya ran away quickly.

An adorable - or fat - *Vatty* came along. He was wrapped in a red cloth and held the hand of his mother Vatty solidly. "Ms. Fat? I mean, madam, do you want..." Kellie but could not finish her sentence, for the Vatty mother scowled at her. They walked away quickly.

"Ehh..." Kellie tapped an *Ossooz* on, "you know where we can sleep? A hotel or something?"

The Ossooz turned, startled.

"Whaaaaaa!" He yelled, "Hessels!" And ran away screaming. "Madam," Kellie said in a voice as if she was sure that this lady that again would run away screaming or cranky and would continue to run, "do you know where we could go? We want a hotel, well forget it... you sure don't know, thank you day."

"No, wait," said the woman ended with a Belgian accent, "there's fanciest hotel of land *Larmana Valariru*." Kellie sighed with relief.

"Fortunately, thanks" Gaya said, sighing. They walked to the hotel. The hotel was dark brown and the inside of the hotel was completely made of marble.

"Oh... woow, chorus, just what I need!" Gaya said happily.
"There's the desk," Kellie said.

They walked to the desk and Kellie looked with horror at the *Googel* behind it. She was quite hairy at her face! She had two horrible tails, the rubber band was a winding worm, so the tails were always different, very high, and then low.

"Ehh... you have a room for us?" asked Gaya scared. "You are even uglier *Magars*. I hate Magars" said the Googel, and Gaya coughed.

"Glad to hear it but you still..." Gaya but could not finish her sentence because Kellie pushed her aside and clenched her fist.

"Listen here gum freak," said Kellie, "we are people, we are soooooo tired and want a room now, otherwise we're out of time!" boasted Kellie.

Suddenly a big ugly woman walked in the door. "Gertalia! Have a room for the guests settled?!" cried the big ugly woman.

"Yes *Urezza*"

"Urezza? Blimey what a name," whispered Kellie at Gaya. "I am the Urezza, who are you?" snapped the woman. Kellie hurled the bag off her back and pulled the phone out with special information with the red Mobic and gold lettering. She typed '*Urezza* 'and there was a very small story:

"Urezza 'is another word for" boss "in the Googels.

"Ehhh... Gaya," Kellie whispered to Gaya, "Urezza is not a name, but that's Googels for 'boss', you know?" Gaya nodded. The Urezza pushed them on to a big green door, there stood "566, MMG.

"What is MMG?" Kellie asked with wide eyes at the Urezza.

"Mini Mugar Guns."

"And that means?" Kellie asked again.

"A Mugar Gun is a piece of chewing gum in your language. So here we have stored guns. Gertalia also chews one of them."

"But why a room full of gun's eh?"

"Now keep on asking questions!" cried the Urezza.

"Uh, the meaning of jorganas?" asked Kellie.

"Jorgana means' 'dunce,'" said the Urezza irritated.

"Oh, thanks," Kellie said.

"20 Celsia!" cried the Urezza. Kellie and Gaya looked at her with big innocent eyes but said nothing.

"Fast like, now!" Commanded the Urezza.

"What ehhh... 20 Celsia?" Gaya is the first who dared to say anything.

"Money, of course, you think the room is free?!" said the Urezza evilly.

"But how much is that?" asked Gaya again.

"I know you people," grinned the Urezza, "my grandmother was one of them, 20 Celsia is 3500 Euro" she grinned.

"Pay or go!" The Urezza pushed them out.

"No money, no room!"

Gaya looked surprised and shocked at Kellie, of course they could not afford it. "Wow what a nice people that were not it," Kellie lied tired but relieved at Gaya.

The More Long

"Phew, that was really pointless and hopeless," grumbled Kellie. They walked back to the open plain, on the very spot where the green pudding seized Vaela.

"Don't you get tired of grumbling?" laughed Gaya.

"No," Kellie said.

"Shall we go exploring, take a swim in the lake or something? It is exciting here!" Gaya said with a huge smile from ear to ear. Kellie raised her right eyebrow.

"Please?" asked Gaya, "I feel like it."

"Why not," Kellie felt bolder.

"Yes!" cried Gaya. She pulled on the reins of Latrez, pranced and drove away.

"Wait for me," said Kellie. They arrived at a large lake.

"This is more…." Said Gaya. "Like a sea," said Kellie staring at the giant lake. Kellie and Gaya got off from Lily and Latrez.

"You stay here, okay?" Kellie stroked the soft white mane of Lily.

"We'll be back again, we just like the lake," said Gaya and ran a bit more, with raised pants.

"Do you like that?" asked Kellie.

"That's some meters deep dude! So your clothes will get wet."

"Not so deep to take a few laps?" Gaya said and ran a little further into the water. She shivered.

"I don't like you in the water!" exclaimed Kellie, "You always get in trouble!"

"Always?" Gaya asked disconsolately.

Kellie deliberately hit her hands over her eyes, "I see nothing," but if down, I'm rescuing you again, Kellie thought to herself.

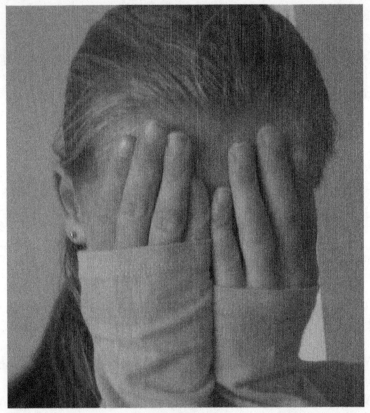

"I see nothing,"

Moments later she opened her eyes again. The water was flat, but no Gaya.

"Gaya? No, huh? No right? Not again!" Kellie looked at the huge lake. "Where are you? This is not funny, Gaya?"

Kellie looked anxiously around. Suddenly the water rose from the lake and burst out a long green beast. It looked like a huge snake. He was green with, yes really, purple dots. It has two dark purple flappers like ears. He had bright blue eyes and a poisonous cobra rings true to his tails. Kellie looked with anxious green eyes in the bright blue eyes of the snake. He had his tail curled up and sat in it, yes, Gaya.

"Kel, help me, please?" She screamed with a pinched voice. Kellie stood petrified. She breathed with long strokes, it was almost inaudible. "Help me!" Screamed Gaya anxiously. Kellie fell forward into the water, she was so stunned. The snake let of Gaya and grabbed Kellie. It dived into the water and even then all was quiet.

Gaya hit her side. She scrambled to her feet and looked at the plain. "Kel? Kel!" she shouted shocked. Then she realized that Kellie had sacrificed herself for her! Gaya dove into the water and had a bamboo stick in her mouth, which was very long. The stick was hollow. So she could breathe while searching for Kellie.

She looked around. The water stung her eyes, but she had to continue. The water was clear, she looked around with narrowed eyes. There she saw a piece of something green with dots disappearing. She swam farther underwater. She was shocked. The stick was not long enough and all the water went into the bamboo stick. She swallowed a lot of water. Gaya swam quickly with one hand up. She coughed and spluttered, looked at the clear water. Suddenly she turned with a jerk and swam to the shore. She picked up the wooden box and pulled out her Mobic, she typed 'more long' in and pressed a small button. Enter. There was a whole story:

More Lang. The more long is a dangerous animal. If they feel threatened, they go ballistic. They swim at 3,000 kilometers per hour. That is unbelievably fast. This is the fastest underwater vehicle that exists. It can reach up to 4000 kilometers per hour. The Vattyns invented this vehicle. They are very proud, they also cost more than 600,000 euros per XL 1000. Only the richest beings can buy this. You cannot just create one. However, the more long is sometimes faster. The longer, the faster. The longest is 1 mile. Then it go six times as fast as an XL 1000. The sea serpent fighter discovered this beast. He was a Magar and was called *Gollino Ervaterry*. The more long has slain him. The more long that has slain him was definitely one kilometer long. And he could be 10 times as hard as the XL 1000. But these more battle is already dead. He was green with purple polka dots, purple flappers like ears and the end of his tail rings, but watch out for his eyes. They are poisonous bright blue. If they watch more than 5 minutes in your face, you cannot talk and see.

Gaya was shocked. Shit! The more long had not looked into her eyes, wait a minute. Green with purple dots, poisonous bright blue eyes. It was the more long that took Kellie.

"Why?" screamed Gaya, "was he nevertheless was dead?!" Suddenly the water rose up again and there was the more long, as a hero in the water, toxic red tongue hanging out. Gaya saw the tongue split into two halves. It was like the tongue of a snake. This tongue was also large.

She ducked back into the water with one of the gadgets of Vaela, a strange figure of stone, as big as a child's hand. The Likkan. The likkan could touch a part and paralyze. She threw it to the more long. He let loose Kellie with a loud cry. She swam to the side and lay there.

Then she hissed, "I'm only doing what I need to do, sorry, this was not intended, I have a chip under my skin that makes me do bad things, get him under my belly from, then again I'm nice, I am driven by *Ellegor,* a malignant Ennoor on this island, sorry, I've been told too much," said the snake, exhausted by the Likkan. Gaya rushed to Kellie. She spluttered and coughed.

"It was not his idea to do this to you, he has a chip!" Gaya pointed with big eyes to the belly of the snake. There was a small device, that blinked red. Kellie ran and gave it a tug, the snake hissed a moment and then looked relieved at his belly. He wriggled into the water again.

"Thank you that you did not kill me," he admitted with his tail wagging with the Likkan that Gaya had thrown.

"is it yours?" Smiled the more long.

"Probably you still need him, you have to kill Ellegor, he really is an evil Ennoor. He thinks he is the boss of this country. He gives all the good animals a chip, so that they should work for him. Turn it off, and you will be rewarded."

Kelly stared at the snake.

"We? Off? Amehoela! I dare not even kick a dead spider, afraid that the stuff that is in the spin goes through my shoe and hit my foot, then I soon become a spider."

"Yeah, but what you did to help your girlfriend was brave Kel," said the snake. Kelly and Gaya looked at him in astonishment.

"How did you know she's called Kellie?" asked Gaya. "I know Vaela, so I know your mission," smiled the snake.

"I'm Ella."

"Are you a female?" asked Gaya.

"Yes," said the snake. "Everyone thinks I'm a male, but I'm a girl. Ella so, Ella said gently.

"Well, thanks for your story, but we try to go on, good luck Ella and thanks," said Kellie a little confused, though she did not know what she thanked her for. And she waved to Ella.

Valariru

"How do you think Ella knew that we know Vaela? Did Ella and Vaela met during her flight home?" Kellie bobbed up and down on Lily's back.

"Can't be," said Gaya, "she went home with that device, the Jooki! So she would have not met Vaela."

"I'm gradually going crazy with all the weird adventures. How did Ella know Vaela? And how do you explain the weird notes?" sighed Kellie. She looked searchingly at Gaya while she stroked Lily's mane.

"Really don't know," murmured Gaya, "you always get notes when you saved me? I did not know that. I can't really explain," said Gaya.

They sat quietly in the back of their horses. Gaya rummaged in her bag. Amazed, she pulled a note out there. It read:

Kel, well saved fat dude! Ella is nice huh? She did not have that chip when I met her. You should disable Ellegor. It's still very different to let anyone be misled by Ellegor. Or how do you get that call it. Do you know where the real Valariru is? Oh no? I will say, it's easy, just follow the route that you are pointing your heart.

Simple right? Tell that to Kel. She has the same feeling as you do because Valariru has magical powers, so that you and Kel will think the same and save and follow each other. Do what your heart tells you, and you defeat Ellegor! Vaela.

Gaya read through the note again incredulously. "What do you got there?" Kelly snatched the paper from Gaya's hands and examined it carefully. When she finished reading, she looked scared at Gaya. "What...?" She stammered.

"I don't know, how Vaela, sent it..." but suddenly there was a loud "beep" and the block, the Gichi appeared from the pockets of Gaya and Kelly. Vaela appeared on the glass display.

"V... V... Vaela," laughed Kelly, "we were talking about you." Vaela looked uncomprehendingly at them. But finally said, "Ellegor is busy, you have to do something! Ella is safe but most animals are not yet!"

"However, the uh..." stuttered Gaya but Vaela interrupted her, she said confidently, "Go! You have everything you need, come on! You can save the entire Valariru Island! I'm sure you can do it. Don't disappoint me!" She hung up and disappeared from the glass screen.

Gaya and Kelly feasted an I-understand-nothing-eye to the Gichi that now was just a small shiny cube. Gaya looked admiringly at her purple cube, and Kelly with her the big green eyes blue hair. "This is crazy," Kelly finally said and put the block in her pocket.

"As if we can do something!" Grumbled Gaya. "But we must not disappoint Vaela."

"Disappoint?" Kelly shouted, "What's wrong with her? She suddenly went away without finishing her story! She left behind strange notes, and now she recommends that we save Valariru without us knowing anything about it! She seemed to be our mother!" she yelled and galloped away.

Gaya shook her dark curls back and forth. "Kel, anyway!" She grinned, "Isn't it cool? We saved Valariru, pooh! We are asked, that's a huge honor?"

"Honor?" Kelly pulled on the reins and Lily stopped, she turned abruptly and looked angrily at Gaya.

"Honor? You put your life on the line for a country with crazy animals and I don't know what comes next, which makes Ellegor awfully dangerous!"

"That's why we have to save these animals," tried Gaya.

"Amehoela," hissed Kelly and drove away. Gaya laughed and drove and chased Kelly.

"What are you laughing anyway?" Kelly looked at Gaya questioningly.

"Nothing," Gaya looked straight ahead, her laughter was briefly stopped. Kelly also looked ahead.

"What would happen if we did not do it?" asked Gaya still staring ahead.

"We get spanked?" chuckled Kelly at Gaya and looked as if it was the funniest joke in the world. Gaya looked at Kelly angrily.

"What exactly do you mean?" asked Gaya.

"Nothing, why?" Kelly got off from Lily and sat on the floor.

"Just," murmured Gaya.

"Gaya, I cannot follow you. Why are you suddenly so serious, then you laugh?" She said.

"Is that right? I'm going to clean out my purse," Gaya said finally.

Kelly had a big smile on her face.
"Has it been 12 hours? Therefore, your face looked like you're just hungry," Kelly said.

Gaya chuckled again. But Kelly did not. She looked straight at Gaya, and suddenly held a piece of paper in the air, there was one sentence written on it:

Follow your heart.

Kelly and Gaya watched with wide eyes, and then stuffed the note. She threw it back in her bag and said, raising his nose, "Very nice hear Gaya."

"What is fun?" asked Gaya. She sat down and picked up a piece of chocolate from her purse. She also gave a piece to Kelly.

"You know best," laughed Kelly.

"No."

"Of course." Kelly pulled the letter out of her purse and gave it to Gaya. They looked at it with wide eyes when she said, "Are you crazy? I did not had it written!"

Kelly burst out laughing, "Yes! Who then? Santa Claus? But wait a minute." Kelly suddenly stopped laughing. She looked anxiously at Gaya.

"One word," she said, "Vaela." Gaya looked at her quizzically and said, "Yes, that's a name?"

"Fascinating," sighed Kelly, "snap it, this is again a note from Vaela! But what the hell are we going to do with this explanation? It is unclear." Kelly threw the note behind her.

Kelly grabbed a packed chewing gum, opened it, took out a piece of chewing gum and chewed it with a considerable momentum in her mouth.

"Yeah, right," nodded Gaya, she stuffed a sandwich in her mouth and swallowed it. Then she picked up a giant marshmallow. She looked at it as if she had landed in a paradise full of candy.

"K-Kel, you must see this!" Gaya proudly showed the bacon. "Ahh... how do you get that Gaya?"

"Just found it! Share?" asked Gaya. Kelly nodded eagerly.

"But back to what we were talking about, Gaya, I also don't understand, we now suddenly have the uh... yeah I don't know, we now suddenly have to be the heroes and stop Ogollor or something?" Kelly looked at Gaya questioningly.

"Ellegor," a voice suddenly improved the name. Kelly watched her Gichi, who already had flown out of her pocket. Vaela reappeared on the glass piece.

"Sorry, but we seemed to be your helpers, you were such a nice girl, and now you want us to be a hero?" Kelly said indignantly. She hit her eyes and grabbed the Gichi firmly in her hand.

"Bye!" She hissed and put the block in her pocket. She tore a large piece of marshmallow and stuffed it in Gaya's mouth. Then she did the same to herself.

"Did you not hear the Gichi squeaked?" asked Gaya.

"No, it was deep in my pocket."

"Why did you mean?" Gaya asked with wide eyes and put the block in her pocket.

"Why? Well because they treat us like slaves. Well, maybe not quite yet, but we seem to be her servants! Don't you think she's going too far Gaya?" asked Kelly sighing.

"Yeah, maybe."

Gaya looked at Kelly and then asked: "do you have a bubblegum?" Kelly nodded and threw a gum in Gaya's hands. She fumbled it open and laid it gently in her mouth. She blew a big bubble and then muttered, "Valariru."

Giant bacon

On the way to the land of death?

"Are we now finally going?" asked Kelly. She looked at Gaya questioningly who was still eating.

"Yep, we go," Gaya swung the bag on her back and hopped on Latrez, then they quickly drove away.

"Hey! Well don't go away fast, wait for me!" Kelly also swung her bag on her back, jumped on and rode Lily chasing Gaya.

When they were next to each other, Gaya said: "We will only stop Ellegor. We'll just do it?"

"What?" Kelly looked irritated. "Are you crazy? You act like it's the most normal thing in the world!"

"Isn't it?" joked Gaya.

"Of course not!" exclaimed Kelly, Gaya said nothing. It was a difficult decision.

"Why do you want to do it?" Kelly asked eventually. "If you are a boss who was as mean as Ellegor, won't you be happy?"

"Who says Ellegor and I are the same? You go, I'll go back to the normal world!" Kelly said. Kelly wanted to pull on the reins to go, but at that moment a piece of paper blew against her face.
"Hey! Who turned off the lights? "Kelly let loose the reins and rolled Lily. The paper flew away and fell at Kelly's feet on the ground. She stood up and looked at the paper carefully. This she read:

Follow your heart and you'll find the right choice
To the real Valariru is a good choice,
If you go there you can tie Ellegor.
So follow your heart, but never your nose,
That's not good.

So anything in abundance.
Provide plenty of food and drink,
And you'll never sink like a brick.
Some people find their own lives important,
While other people's lives (at risk) are wiped out
From the past, now is the present.
Care for the demise of Ellegor and the right way you will see,
If you do this, you get me a ten out of ten. Vaela.

Kelly's eyes were finally opened. She suddenly understood that it was important that Ellegor was slain. "Vaela is right, we need to save lives of others, and we'll go to the land of death!"

"What?" cried Gaya. "On the way to the land of death?"

Discover everything worth

"Yes, what else?" Kelly looked at Gaya puzzled, "you wanted to do it badly?"

"Ehhh..." Gaya fingered the reins.

"Yes, but ehhh... I understand you not, at first you did not want!"

Kelly looked at her and grinned, "Perhaps you're afraid? You and your big mouth, "she smiled. Gaya looked at her with large animated eyes.

"I am not," she stammered, "I'm not afraid, but..." she looked at the sky, "tired."

"Tired?" Kelly raised her eyebrow. "Right Now? So suddenly?"

Gaya nodded vigorously, "and I'm frustrated... ehh, Ha," she laughed fake.

"Whatever," Kelly looked ahead and pointed to a broad mountain in the distance. She looked with glittering big eyes to the mountain, "there we go."

Gaya looked anxiously at the mountain. "Okay," she took a deep breath and galloped down the path straight to the mountain in the distance. A proud smile appeared on Kelly's face. She pulled Lily's rein. Lily pranced and she drove away fast.

Kelly looked at Gaya with wide eyes, "ehh... we must continue what we are doing here?"

"Hello, what else? You wanted it anyway? "asked Gaya nipping.

"Yes, but... ok come with me!" Kelly picked up the box Jooki, then she exclaimed, "On top of the mountain! Gaya, Latrez, LILY and Kelly, NOW!" She flew into the air and disappeared.

Moments later, they were on top of the mountain.

"Okay! Smart enough," Gaya said staring at a huge and high house with ridiculous story. The house was completely made of ice. There were major points on top, and there floated a large silver and gold lamps.

Finally Kelly said sarcastically, "This is too weird." She walked to the large door, Gaya rang six times. Even the ring that hung on the door was made of ice. The ring was in the form of an Ennoorkop. Of course because Ellegor was Ennoor.

First you heard nothing, only the rustle of the wind, but then the big doors opened. There appeared a little girl Munka.

"Hello, what are you doing here? And what are you?" The Munka squeezed her eyes.

"We come for Ellegor and we are just people. This seems like a house of a nasty bitter villain, so where is he?" Kelly took a step on the threshold that was suddenly in purple flames.

"What are you planning? Well?" Said the Munka now angry.

"We are people, we would like to speak to Ellegor, "Gaya said, smiling, and gave Kelly an unnoticed kicked in her shin. Kelly rubbed her leg and looked angrily at Gaya.

"What happened?" She snarled softly.

"In that case," the Munka looked at them and grinned, "Come in, Ellegor sits on the 530th floor.

Kelly and Gaya got insecure on the doorstep. But the fire was extinguished. They walked the chilly corridor. Gaya looked startled. They heard only a drop of the wall.

"Gaya, are you okay? The Munka has run long enough," laughed Kelly.

Gaya ran to Kelly uncertainly, "Are you going to do it?" She asked scared.

"Duh, no, I am the spirit of the Evil Elves, haha!" Kelly said, grinning.

They walked on. "How do you really know how to walk?" Gaya asked Kelly with wide eyes.

"She has just explained to me." Kelly said to Gaya and continued walking until they reached something that looked like an elevator made of black marble.

"What now?" Gaya looked at Kelly questioningly.

"Logically, we ride it?" Kelly pushed a button, the size of a thick round baby elephant. Made of stone.

"Then press?" asked Gaya surprised.

Kelly nodded. They pushed, but there was no movement.

"Again!" screamed Kelly. She pressed the big button, but nothing happened again.

"I give up," said Gaya, she hit her eyes, so she suddenly saw a white stone, between all that black marble fell. She stood on it. The large knob suddenly went inside, all the stones moved and then flew into the air. They fell right down in a heap.

For them it was a big swing. It was no elevator. Kelly watched Gaya watched with wide eyes. She smiled triumphantly.

"Come on, don't be so dramatic," said Kelly nipping. Gaya took off her coat and laid it on the ground. She sat down, took off and shot into the tunnel.

"Wait for me!" cried Kelly, but she did not removed her coat and just jumped into the tunnel. She slid hundreds of meters down. Then she fell into a huge purple container. There was 528th floor in a bright blue sign, which was all lit up, and the whole floor was of pure white marble.

"Well, what now?" asked Gaya.

Kelly scrambled out of the bin and finally said, "you see that sign or not? We still have two floors up."

"But you noticed that?" Gaya dropped her shoulders liked stunned bags, "we went into a tunnel down! These are from top to bottom! The top floor is number 1. It is all around! The first number, number 1, above, and the last number, number 530, is the lowest!" Kelly stared at Gaya as if she had just said something terribly disordered.

"Aye," said Kelly, "perfect information. So we need more down?"

"Exactly," nodded Gaya.

Moments later, she still walked through the white corridor and suddenly out of nowhere Gaya said, "You know Kel, you know how we got here without us knowing the way?"

Kelly turned with a jerk and shrugged.

"Don't be silly! This is serious!"

"Well, well, what do you mean?" asked Kelly.

"Ehh... you remember that piece of paper? Follow your heart? Or so? That you got?"

Kelly nodded. "That is Vaela! She sent notes to help us! She predicted the future!"

Kelly looked at Gaya dumbfounded "that can't..." she said as if she had a hot potato in her throat, "no, it cannot!"

"Well?" cried Gaya. They stayed a few minutes staring at each other.

"No," whispered Kelly, "there is still no money falling from the sky?" She said, "Because that's hogwash."

"That might not be, but you still believe in all those people who called to yell on the street that Valariru exist, right? Well?" screamed Gaya.

Kelly nodded, "You're right," she said, "or basically NO, you did not, it cannot!" She cried, "Listen Gaya, I decided to beat Ellegor. Vaela has me convinced of that, but I really don't believe in all that crap around it! I still cannot conjure it?!"

And while Kelly said that, suddenly a huge flame shot from her hand. She fell back with a bang. Gaya stared at her incredulously. "No..." she said, "this cannot be!"

Ellegor

"That was nothing though," tried Kelly.

"Welles, I saw it right? It was a flame! Did you notice that? This world is bewitched," screamed Gaya scared.

"Bewitched?" said Kelly, "with monsters?" Kelly pulled on a rod sticking out of the wall. The rod at the same time went down. Gaya fell in a huge hole that had appeared. Kelly dangled from the rod above the hole, her hands did not like it and when she fell in depth. They came with a soft blow up on the floor, the floor was now not of marble, it was just a soft red rug. She saw a huge door, 16 times as large as normal doors. And there was a big Ennoorkop on, it, like the door outside.

"Okay," said Gaya exhausted. She grabbed the doorknob (which was rather high), but at the same time it was made of ice!

Kelly looked at Gaya incredulously, "I told you so?" said Gaya, "this is a magic world, such strange things happen, I can just do magic and make ice cream!"

"Probably, but can you get that door open? It is now on ice, now you cannot push it down."

Gaya yanked on the doorknob, but it was no use, it would not go down. Gaya looked at Kelly, she said, "do that flame of fire again!"

"I cannot, I don't know how I did that!" Kelly kept her hand on the knob. It became hot and melted.

"Push the door open quickly, otherwise there is no button anymore!" Grumbled Kelly.

"Ehh..." Gaya looked at her anxiously, "we now in Ellegor's house."

"So what?" snapped Kelly.

Gaya pushed the door open. There stood Ellegor. He looked at them and grinned. Ellegor looked like a wilted and dried plants that needed a lot of water and white short hair. His face was pale and seemed to put up with a lot of black makeup. His long teeth were ugly and yellow. He was also very long, longer than two meters and skinny. Ellegor had a black suit, but his pants were too short and the sleeves too.

"You are Gaya and Kelly I suppose?" He laughed. Gaya fell backwards.

"How do you know that?" cried Kelly.

"How do I know? Oh, Hessels are really stupid!" He laughed loudly.

Kelly had a plan for her newly discovered magic hands. She ran up to him and wanted her hand against his face so that he would burn. Kelly hit her hand against his face, but nothing happened. Kelly looked surprised, "why..."

"Do you really think that's how I'll die? Crushed by a few handfuls of yours? I am ELLEGOR!" He cried, and laughed. He grabbed her arm. Kelly screamed. It felt like thousands of nettles to her body, especially her arm.

"So," he finally let go. Kelly grabbed her arm, it burned terribly. Gaya had to invent something. She finally stood up and hit the wall, so that everywhere razor sharp icicles would come to drop. But when she attempted, Ellegor snapped his fingers and all the icicles disappeared.

Out of nowhere a big boxing glove came out of the wall and hit Gaya hard against her head. Kelly stood up and pointed to the chair of Ellegor which was suddenly on fire. "You think you can handle me, eh?" He suddenly flew into the air, and just kept floating.

Still tormented by the thought Kelly said, "How do you know Vaela?" She demanded.

"Her parents," he cried, "they have ruined my life. My father was an inventor. He had made a kind Jooki, but her father corrected him. He got all the fame and my parents had no money. We were poor. My father was not good enough and was dismissed as a professor, and I sat with Vaela in the classroom. The whole class always called out, 'there you have that son of the failed professor.' You would have found that nice."

Kelly swallowed and muttered. "He is very angry." With his eyes he let a chair fly in the air and threw to Gaya and Kelly and laughed." But now I'm back and will be ruler over Valariru!" Ellegor floated and looked at himself in a mirror. He laughed.

"He is really scary," Gaya mumbled, her eyes wide.

"Gaya, go!" Kelly suddenly whispered, "Now!"

Jenny

"Get out!" cried Gaya now.

Ellegor let himself be distracted by his own reflection and thus Kelly and Gaya managed to escape. They ran to an open window and jumped out.

Fortunately, they had escaped! They outsmarted Ellegor.

"That was pointless. After everything we've done to get there," Gaya said bitterly.

"The worst thing is," Kelly sighed and stroked Lily's mane, "we need more time. Because of Vaela we let run him away!"

"Shoo!" Gaya pulled Latrez's rein. They stopped, "We have to murder him!" She said indignantly.

"So," snapped Kelly at Gaya, "we cannot do it? You know what? As she says he is so bad."

"Yes, that's true, you're right, we'll stop. We leave the job to Vaela!"

Still shaking from the pain and the fear, they rode. "Let's go there," Kelly pointed to a lake, "then we can drink and eat." They drove to the lake, and Lily and Latrez jumped.

"What do we start?" Gaya was completely in her sack and licked her lips. She picked up a bag of candies and gummies. She put a big yellow rubber in her mouth and finally said, smacking "how can we actually go back home?"

Kelly almost choked in her chocolate. "Yes!" She cried and swallowed her chocolate piece through, "we did not even know how we got here!" She cried out, startled.

"We have to go figure it out," said Gaya calmly.

"Hey, how do you stay so calm? We have to go back home." Kelly was angry.

"How come? Surely we can still stay here? Ellegor is not that bad, "suggested Gaya.

"Yup? Yes you think? Well then you're allowed to stay beautiful, but I go to Mom and Dad, home to Miu and Angel. And Bora, our dear darling long haired dog!" Kelly said.

"Oh yeah... those sweet creatures of us..." Gaya let the bread fall out of her mouth, the slice of cheese fell with a slob sound like the pancake Kelly dropped in the water. The bread fell into the grass.

"I had forgotten for a moment...... but now that you mention it..."

"Forgotten?" cried out Kelly surprised, "how could you forget them?"

Gaya shrugged.

"Sorry," she began to sob softly, tired of all the events.

"Tell that to them," muttered Kelly. She stepped on Lily and drove away.

Gaya took the sandwich out of the grass. She swallowed it and picked up the plastic bag with the sandwich in it and stuffed it in her bag. Suddenly she heard a huge scream. She jumped on Latrez and drove away. Straight for the screams. When she looked, she could not believe what she saw. There was a huge and ugly beast, a troll. His big fat body was green and he had a red vest and too small holes in his head that turned up to be ears but its ugly bald head was as small as a football. He had bulging eyes that were reminiscent of Ping-Pong balls and he got one eye higher than the other. He had a sloppy mouth without teeth. He had a sledgehammer in his hand and his little nose grew long hair.

Gaya looked at the big ugly troll and shivered from the foul beast. "Aaahhhh!" screamed Gaya.

Kelly was scared on the ground. The ugly beast had his sledgehammer above his head and waved threateningly at Kelly. Gaya screamed. He dropped his sledgehammer down, missing Kelly a millimeter.

"Woow," she screamed, but that was not all, he tried again. They fled in a tree. The ugly beast did not see them, because he was almost blind, but his other senses were better. He looked around and feeling, but saw their really not. Kelly grabbed her purse from the wooden box, quickly grabbed the red Mobic and typed: 'ugly troll' in. This came to be:

No information found for "ugly troll."

Kelly sighed, "what's it called then? Ugly sucker with sledgehammer?" She said a little too hard. The ugly beast heard her and swung the sledgehammer above his head, he threw his hammer to where Kelly and Gaya sat. They let out a cry scared.

"Shit," Gaya said in a whisper.

"Yuck," Kelly said. She dived aside and attacked both from the tree, hit the breaker off a branch, which fell exactly on Kelly.

"Ouch!" She screamed and pushed with difficulty the branch aside, scribbled back and screamed,

"AAAAHHHH" Hammer hurtled down and hit her with just the stem. She fell to the ground in pain. Gaya ran to her and pulled her up, threw her on Lily and pulled herself to Lily's reins so they could go straight away. They galloped away, Latrez behind them.

When she was a few kilometers away from the ugly beast and were sure that they were safe, grabbed Gaya and Kelly jumped off from Lily and laid her on the ground. Kelly sat down.

"My head hurts," she muttered and groaned and hit her hand to her head.

"Ouch!" She screamed. She looked at her hand and saw that there was a little blood.

"Stupid troll," she muttered. She grabbed the box from the sheet and then pressed on the stalk. The drop fell down on her wound, which began to give light, and then again gave all colors. The wound was healed.

Suddenly a kind of snake wriggled towards them, he was not as big as an ordinary snake, about 50 cm long.

"No, not again," sighed Gaya, she was already backing out, but the snake remained. Suddenly it opened its mouth and a small flame came out. It was only a trickle, or whatever you call it. Kelly quickly grabbed an electrical pocketknife that did everything naturally. She wanted to press the button when suddenly the snake yawned and lay down.

"Ah... what a run, a real sweetheart," squeaked Kelly. She stretched her arm toward the creature that was now snoring.

"Stop," Gaya grabbed Kelly's her arm, "it's probably a trap, you grab him and that diabolical beast grabs you," said Gaya.

"Devil?" smiled Kelly, "Sometimes you're a real nightmare," she teased, stooped down to the creature and picked it up.

Gaya squeezed her eyes shut and said, "I don't want to see it."

"Ahhhhh!" squeaked Kelly. Gaya opened her eyes; Kelly was stroking the beast. "He's so cute." Kelly looked with loving eyes to the tube. He looked with big brown eyes at Kelly.

"Sorry, dear tube." Kelly put the tube into the grass. "I must go." She jumped up at Lily.

Gaya nodded, glad that Kelly did not take the snake. They drove on. But did not notice that the snake was stuck on Lily's leg. Lily pranced and tried to shake off the snake but the serpent held tight. Kelly fell and lay in the damp grass.

"Yuck, this is just a new pair of pants," grumbled Kelly.

"You well eh?" Laughed Gaya. Kelly stood up and looked at her pants, which had become a little wet.

"Why did you do that?" Grumbled Kelly to Lily, Lily watched her left hind leg. "Oooooh! Look who's here." Kelly took the snake from Lily's leg. "Come down snake but, what are you doing poopy here?" She asked, holding the tube in the air. "I'll take you," laughed Kelly.

Gaya looked at her with wide eyes. "WHAT, why?" she screamed, and almost fell off Latrez herself.

"Yes," laughed Kelly, "I take her. She is sooooo sweet!"

"How do you know it's a she?" Demanded Gaya and looked at the bottom of the snake.

"Ehh... I cannot see it, well, I'll just take it." Kelly stepped on Lily and looked at the beast.
"Jenny."

"Jenny? Jenny?" cried Gaya.

"Yes, what's wrong with that? Jenny."

"That... that... that... is a snake! Our niece is Jenna!"

"Yes, Jenna. Not Jenny."

"Blimey," sighed Gaya and pulled on Latrez's reins. "Keep that thing away from me and keep it in your bag. I hope I have been clear. Let's move on. According to me, the mountains, or who Ellegor you brains have been affected!"

Thrill

"Well, where are we going?" Kelly pointed to a wide path away, and then to a thin narrow frizzy path with nettles beside it.

"What is the best path?"

"I don't know." Gaya shrugged. Jenny slid along the arm of Kelly down and wriggled to the wide path. She pointed at the tip of its tail to the path.

"Good, then we take the wide path," laughed Kelly, "are you happy with it."

"Yeah! If that small unhygienic reptile says we should go there, I suppose so that it is nice the other way," protested Gaya.

"Come on Gaya," soothed Kelly, "we can surely listen to Jenny? Maybe she's right."

"Gee, that would be something to say," Gaya said bitterly. She drove through the thin narrow path.

"Sorry Jen, but if Gaya is going to do that, I have to follow her, I have no choice, I cannot let her perish on that narrow path." Jenny scrambled from Lily's leg to her back and sat in Kelly's backpack. They drove through the narrow path between the trees. When Kelly saw Gaya driving faster she drive fast until she rode beside her.

"Gaya, why are you still so worried?"

"Because that dumb beast of yours bullying! It probably has such a chip as Ella had. I believe nothing like that Jenny may indicate where to go, you trust a snake?"

Kelly scowled at her, "yes why not, we still have some...." Kelly broke a branch off.

"It's a very dark way, don't you think?" Gaya nodded.

Kelly kept the branch firmly in her hand. It began to glow red and was suddenly hot, and began to burn. Almost the entire path was now enlightened.

"So convenient anyway, with Vaela's tricks! Let's move on," Kelly said. But Lily and Latrez were too tired to begin. Kelly and Gaya jumped from their horses to rest.

"There is a cottage," Kelly pointed to a wooden shack nearby. She walked there. Cracking the door opened, there sat an old woman. It looked like a man, a real man. Kelly was startled.

"Hello ma'am. Sorry, but can we rest here for a minute? You're the only person we have well, come across."

"Sit down kinders, yes that's because Valariru has only Chanana's," said the old woman. Kelly grabbed the Mobic Chanana and typed in. This came to be:

'Chanana's "means to Beings of Valariru

.

Chanana may be different beings. A Chanaan could be: an Ennoor. Ellegor is one of them, a Magar, a Uluz a Chessova a Googel, or Vatty. There are still more Chanana such as: the dreaded Lentotore. Who has just discovered a Magar. The discoverer called: Kafut Blue Blood. A Lentotore looks like this: it's a big ugly troll with a sledgehammer in his hand, totally green, a small head with a large body, they have different types of jackets, usually blue or red, large Ping-Pong eyes, a small nose with large nostrils. Beware of Lentotores, because they are very dangerous. You can recognize a baby Lentotores with all blue, green vest, always, and a big nose, small nostrils, and small oval eyes. These are so Chanana programs; different kinds of creatures.

Kelly nodded. "Sorry ma'am, we have not even imagined. This is Gaya," Kelly pointed to Gaya. "And I'm Kelly, these are our horses. My horse is Lily. Lily come on over here!" exclaimed Kelly.

The white horse came and went in a corner of the room to defecate. "This is so, Lily!" screamed Kelly suddenly, when she saw that Lily had dropped a huge turd.

"A fresh horse, I like that." The old woman nodded. Kelly and Gaya attacked the stench of order and were green as lettuce. Kelly was then red as a tomato of anger, while the woman just stared into her rocking chair thoughtfully at Lily and occasionally nodded and said, "Ah, perfect, perfect..." and then it was another thing to not understand. Gaya ran to the window, pulled the lever to open the window Thus, the stench finally pulled away.

"Sorry, where were we?" Kelly always made a motion as if she could vomit at any moment.

"Does not hear of that turd," the woman said.

"This is my horse Latrez, I hope that he has already given out to the slugs and worms their daily needs," Gaya said, blushing. Latrez also entered, as Gaya thought that she was going to do a pee, but that was not so lucky. "This is my snake Jenny," said Kelly and opened her purse. Jenny slipped out.
"What a beautiful, a South Valariruse Magaarninaz.

"Ehh... a what?" asked Kelly, "it's just a snake?"

"No, no child, this is a real Magaarninaz. A real one. She is just as beautiful as Choenitzy"

"May I ask who Choenitzy is?" Kelly raised her eyebrow.

"My Valariruse kingfisher, she is shy, so be gentle."

Kelly and Gaya nodded suspiciously, "okay."

"Choeny!" cried the woman, "Oh, and I'm Sascha, Sascha Mitania Gorza Mataria."

86

"Oo, ehh... we will remember it," lied Kelly whistling and looked at the wall.

"Call me Sascha." Suddenly, around the corner, a skittish white kingfisher flew. His wings were gray. He had three white hairs, and gray on his head, which stuck all three at the other side. He was nice and cute to see.

"Choenitzy, come," Sascha waved to the beast, but in vain.

"It does not matter, we need to find that Kafut Blue Bloods," Kelly said.

"Who is that?" asked Gaya. Kelly gave the Mobic to Gaya and let her read the information.

"Crazy," she muttered.

"Blue Bloods Kafut huh?" Asked Sascha, "I know him, he is the boss of a very famous Chanana Journal. Extreme Valariru Information. They pay a fortune to a stupid subscription to that magazine. I know here, one such sheet it costs half Celsia."

"Sure, but how much is that in people money, ehh... Euro?" asked Gaya.

"That is 85.00 euro and 50 cents, kid. 85.50."

"How expensive is such a plan?" asked Kelly eagerly.

"5 Celsia," Sascha whispered.

"How much is that?" asked Kelly,

"I don't count." Sascha leaned forward a little from her chair and whispered again, "That is 855 euros," she nodded slowly and dropped back again in the armchair bags. "Too bad that we have not," said Kelly.

"How come? Would you like a stupid magazine?"

"Yes," grinned Kelly, "thinking of Gaya." The big grin on her face was even greater.

"Through Thinking?" Gaya raised her eyebrow. Kelly sighed. "If we all come to know what is happening here, we will know in no time how to beat Ellegor. Convenient isn't it?" Gaya's smiled.

"To beat Ellegor? You?" Sascha stood.

"Only if you have the right powers. The human world have no powers, but Valariru is magical. Anything goes, any real person who lives here has powers."

"Living more people?" asked Kelly.

"No," said Sascha, "unfortunately not, I and now with you there. You two are the only one who made it. I was dragged here by a Magar, He was just in the human world, took me, and I got powers. I was young, I've lived here since I was 6th. I don't know any better."

Kelly suddenly saw that Sascha had no real tongue, but it was a snake tongue. She slithered it out of her mouth fast, but then disappeared again.

Gaya seemed not to notice. "Gaya" Kelly whispered in Gaya's ear, "I..."

But Kelly paused because Sascha looked at her smiling. Kelly saw something she had never seen before. Sascha had pointy teeth.

"What child?" She asked, and smiled even wider. It was kind of scary like Dracula's teeth glistening in the sun. They shone like diamonds, were sharp as knives, and Kelly was convinced that it could even cut through steel.

"Ehh nothing," she said slowly. Choenitzy suddenly came flying. She grabbed her hair and pulled Sascha hard. Kelly and Gaya's faces paled.

It turned out to be a wig! Under the wig were hidden huge flappers, like Ella had, they were just sharper and smaller. In the middle of her forehead, between the two flappers sat a huge green dot. Which was just as sharp as her teeth. It looked like a real tooth, and very large.

"Children, it's not what you think," said Sascha, but her voice suddenly sounded as though she was a crow.

"Gaya, get out of here," whispered Kelly, "Sascha is not a man!" She ran to the door but it was locked.

"Choenitzy what have you done?" shouted Sascha and looked at the bird, "I will..."

"No!" screamed Gaya, when Sascha jumped on the bird. She pressed her hand against Sasha's hand, which was as cold as ice.

"Brat," shrieked Sascha. She clutched at Gaya's arm, but she dodged. Kelly jumped off at Sascha.
"I have the Air force, you cannot compete here," she screamed and swung her arms. The air whistled at them, they were pressed hard against the wall and also Lily, Latrez, Jenny and Choenitzy.

"You have beaten the last hour, little sucker! Choenitzy, I thought you knew better. It's a shame that such a sweet little bird! Now I have to kill you anyway. Sorry, but it's your own fault! You will be able to finish this trip!"

"You don't Sascha!" screamed Kelly. She pressed her hand against the door, which was hot and just went up in flames, and when the door was gone. Kelly, Gaya, Jenny, Lily Latrez, and also Choenitzy flew out. Sascha flew off the path until they cannot see Sascha anymore. Success!

Kafut Blue Bloods

Gaya sat down slowly.

"What... what... happened? My head!" She rubbed her head.

"Kelly?" asked Gaya.

Kelly lay unconscious on the ground.

"Oo, yeah, I remember."

Gaya stood up and wiped the gravel of her pants and jacket. "Sascha, Where is Choenitzy?"

Gaya looked around and saw Kelly.

"What? Man, crikey! I have a headache! What happened? I sometimes rotated in a cement mixer?"

She stood with difficulty and smoothed her hair back.

"Where is Choenitzy?" Gaya asked Kelly and shook her jacket back and forth.

"I don't know. I have a headache, I believe she's fallen beside my bag. Somewhere my bag flew off my back. Can look for my bag? Look, there she is."

Gaya rushed to Choenitzy. She lifted her and looked at her. "Choenitzy?" The bird opened his eyes and looked at Gaya scared. She stood up, put the animal in her backpack, and went up Latrez.

"Shall we?" Kelly nodded. She took Jenny and laid her on her shoulder. Then she went to Lily and they drove off.

"What do you want?" Gaya pulled out a bag of candy, "a gummie or liquorice?"

"Find out yourself enough," Kelly said.
"What are you so pissed off at?" Asked Gaya.

"We have only just escaped a fake bitch. We're in a country with only beasts who want us dead. We don't know how to return home. Is there any reason to put a smile on someone's face?" Kelly said to Gaya.

"Ehh... no..."

"Well then," muttered Kelly, she looked ahead.

"Hey look there, a house," said Gaya and pointed to a huge house of pink marble, big as a castle.

"House" Kelly stared at the thing and pulled her eyebrow. "That thing is like a country so big!"

"Well don't overdo Kel," Gaya said still staring at the giant house. "Shall we go?"

They drove to the enormous house. "Wow..." said Kelly, "I cannot believe this..."

"A house is..." Gaya finished the sentence.

"Exactly..." Kelly Gaya and jumped off their horses.

"Yes!" Muttered Gaya. She stretched as far as she could from her arm to reach the doorknob, but the door was 20 meters high, and the handle was 10 meters high.

"Duh!" Kelly turned her eyes, "was it 9 feet?" Suddenly the huge doors swung open by itself. There was a huge giant, he had a short goatee. Apparently he was young. He had short curly hair with a golf cap and carried a huge green pack. This fits exactly with the green doors. And underneath was a purple T-shirt.

"Are you Mr. Kafut? Ehh... Blue Blood?" asked Gaya.

"Of course not," said Kelly, "this is a giant or something, Kafut Blue Blood is an Ennoor, like Ellegor, and yet he was also a lot smaller?"

"Oo, yeah, sorry, I'm not so good at remembering names of this rather idiotic world."

"No! Kafut a Magar," roared the giant, the trees shook and Kelly, who was as small as an ant looked at giant's eyes. Gaya had struggled to remain still when the giant roared hard.

"Sorry," he said a little softer, everything was shaking again. Then he whispered.

"Do you know Kafut?" Kelly asked eagerly.

"What?" Asked the giant.

"Do you work for Kafut?" shouted Kelly.

"Yes, how do you know?"
"I guess but whatever," Kelly shouted again, otherwise the giant could not hear her.

"Come along with me," he whispered, and still had Kelly struggled to remain standing.

"Okay, bring us to Kafut?" asked Gaya.

"Who else?" asked the friendly giant, "I don't know so many things. Only Ellegor, and yes, I know the best."

"What do you mean you know Ellegor?" asked Gaya, "you sometimes work for him?" She stepped back and clung to a tree.

"In the past, a moment, but for not anymore. He was much too dangerous," said the giant, and even shuddered. It seemed as if he thereby caused an earthquake; the ground was shaking like crazy. Kelly clung squeaking onto Lily.

"Sorry," said the giant, "I will have nothing more to say, oops now I say this, and this..."

"Jaha" Kelly shouted, "Bring us now to Blue Blood!"

"Good," nodded the giant and he stepped into the huge doors. "Ehh... Mr. Giant," stammered Gaya, "How high are these doors anyway?"

"About 20 meters, I pass there just underneath and the handle is 10 meters."

"So Kel," said Gaya, "you guessed it, you still thought it was 9 feet?"

"That I did not say," Kelly said.

"Well, you said," Duh, you're not a 9 meter? So when you said it."

"Yes, but I meant that you surely are no 9 meters?!" Kelly replied. Fortunately the giant interrupted the bickering girls.

"I don't like that stupid chatter of girls. Here, press this call, I go to the lobby. You just come along. Kafut's a good fellow, but sometimes he gets overwrought so be nice and quiet."

The giant marched away, and the house was shaking like 1000 drills. Or actually castle. Kelly fell again. Lily whinnied and reared Latrez so it just seemed like the giant talked.

"A double earthquake!" Kelly pressed her hands against her ears, "it should now already be stopped? Earthquake that lasts for hours! How can that be?"

"I don't know!" Shouted Gaya with her hands also pressed against her ears, the wall was shaking so that pieces of rock fell down and some clattered broken.

"Let's quickly go inside!" cried Kelly.

"Is the door locked?"
"No, look, it is still ajar," cried Gaya.

Kelly kicked at the door, pressed her hands against her ears and pushed Latrez inside. Jenny was on her shoulder and squirmed restlessly up and down. Gaya ran inside, followed by Latrez. Suddenly it was very quiet and peaceful, the earth trembled no more.

"Hello?" Gaya looked anxiously toward the ground.

"Wait," Kelly looked at the wall, she touched her hand to the wall.

"Fire..." she tried, but the wall did not glowed not red.

"Come on..." she whispered. But the ceiling was just white. "I cannot believe it," grumbled Kelly, she scratched her head.

"Gaya, I already know what the problem is. I believe, that wall is certainly not concrete, it's a different kind of limestone, very crazy stuff, maybe something special from Valariru. Don't you think? Otherwise it could not stand that earthquake and against my fire."

"Yes, that is true." Gaya said. Meanwhile Choenitzy pulled off her backpack and shook the creature together.

"Hello?" Gaya said anxiously. Choenitzy looked at her with tired eyes, "what?"

94

"Hush, that witch is gone," Gaya reassured Choenitzy.

"Here Blue Blood is certainly not," muttered Kelly. "Then we can go again, in any case."

"No!" Gaya said, "It's so quiet here, outside the earth trembles. Let's just stay here!"

Gaya suddenly saw a big red chair out of corner of her eye. He stood with his back towards them.

"Welcome," suddenly said a shrill voice. The chair turned around. And there was a kind of man. He seemed to be different. Kelly understood nothing. "Ehh... ehh... are you a human being?"

"No girl, girl. Hessels don't survive here. I, the great, am a Magar."

"Oh, yeah, that was in our Mobic. Well, you can spend some time on this habitat, about Valariru? "
"Certainly children," he said. The Magar looked just 20. He had a little oblique hanging blond curls and a white shirt with a rather strange pants. He had dark black boots.

"Are you Kafut?" asked Kelly hesitantly.

"Yes, definitely! Who else should I be? Such a smart guy like me does not exist! But, uh... well, enough about me, who are you?" He rattled on.

"I uh... Kelly," said Kelly with raised lip.

"And I'm Gaya," Gaya said gently.

Kelly turned and made strange noises and put her finger in her mouth. But once Kafut looked at her strangely, she turned and looked at him with friendly eyes.

"Well," he said and snapped his fingers.

Suddenly there came out two Uluzen. They were carrying chairs and put them behind Kelly and Gaya. They pushed the girls back and waddled away immediately. Kelly and Gaya and flopped down on the chairs and Kafut began: "Well, what are you asking?"

"Ehh... wait a minute, mister," moaned Kelly, she was quite painful in the chair. Her head was on the right handrail and her left leg was over the back. Her right leg was lying dazed on the ground. When she was decent again, she looked cheerful to others.

"At the beginning but hear," Kelly said.

"Yeah, where were we?" asked Kafut and watched with a bored face on his watch.

"Well, my question first," cried Kelly, she stuck her finger in the air.

"We are not in school Madame Kelly and moreover there's just the two of us."

"Don't call me Madame," protested Kelly, "but hey, why does the earth began to tremble so?"

"Good question," grinned Kafut, "so does the earth again, as our Ellegor weather strikes. An innocent being to leave the life..."

"Oh no, how awful!" screamed Gaya and Kelly concurrently.

"But we have saved more long Valariru a chip" Gaya said proudly.

"What more long? There are many more snakes here."

"That was Ella!" Kelly said.

"Ella?! Ella?! The old more long? Actually, quite a distance away? But she still was long dead?"

"Yes, everyone thinks," said Kelly, and shrugged, "but it is not so."

"No," said Kafut stunned. "Any more questions?"

"Yes, a lot, why we do have forces in this country?"

"In Valariru you always have forces, remember that," whispered Kafut.

"Do you know Sascha?"

"Sascha? Yes, you have fought her?"

"Yes..." Kelly whispered, "Is that really...? It is important...? But they attacked us and..."

"Hush," soothed Kafut, "no, that's just very good of you! That means you are not like the other Hessels here. They did not make it to Sascha. It is perhaps because the successor of the poor Ellegor. Why she's so good..."

"Oh dear... ..Last question sir Kafut. Why should we murder that horrible creature Ellegor?"

"Well, fate has chosen you to do it. You were smart to fight Sasha off so that's why you can beat Ellegor. Then you save everything and everyone in Valariru."

"But that's madness!" Kelly shouted suddenly, "we cannot do it yet!"

"Aha! Wait... but you try and you'll see" Kafut grabbed a can from his drawer, it said SUPERGEYOXIDE. Trendiest DRINK OF VALARIRU. Kelly grabbed the can, held it in her hand and waited. She hoped just it then it did not work so Kafut could send them home. But that was too much hoped that the tin melted.

"Chips," muttered Kelly, "Ouch! Ouch!" She reached for her hand.

"Kafut why does it hurt?!" she screamed.

"It means you can do more than this. Such a can is not enough for you, you have more in you than just melt a tin. From the outside you don't appear as strong, but inside it works very well with you, and there is the opposite! You are a warrior, you can use it Kelly. Listen to my words. Gaya, now you."

He threw the same can to her.

"Wow, you drink a lot of that stuff," muttered Gaya. Kafut coughed. "Good, good," muttered Gaya. She picked up the can and held it firmly in her hand. It was first a little cold. But then came a layer of ice around it, then another, and another, until Gaya dropped the tin. Now it was nine times as thick. Gaya also grabbed her hand, "ouch, ouch! I did it too!" She screamed.

Kelly stood up. Her pain was gone. Moments later, Gaya stood.

"Well done girls, you are ready for it," said Kafut happy.

"We also have pets," said Kelly, to talk about something else.

"Yes, I know, Latrez, Lily, Jenny and the newcomer Choenitzy."

"How did you know?"

"Just, just, I still know everything. But now you must return."

"But we don't even know where to go," said Kelly.
"You know," said Kafut, he gave Kelly a small crumpled piece of paper. Suddenly he was gone.

Lacrazitos River

Gaya shuddered. The thought of yet another Vaela-paper chased the true meaning of fear.

"What is it?" Gaya leaned over to Kelly's shoulder to see what was there. Annoyed - by some paper again - Kelly folded the paper. This stood in curled letters:

Kelly and Gaya, You have kicked wonderful so far. Very good. Did you see Ellegor? Oh no? We Hessels, are a miraculous kind. But he is also common! Crush Ellegor. Crush him. Vaela

"Gosh first Vaela was still nice, but now it seems she is our dismal teacher of German lessons," Kelly said with disgust and tore the letter into a thousand pieces.

"What a stupid and strange letter that was," murmured Gaya, "everything here is strange, I still don't understand why I'm awake," she gave herself a slap against her sleep. "Ouch!" She shrieked, "That hurt."

"I think you are awake, I'll just help you remember it?" Grinned Kelly, and she yanked at Gaya's hair.

"Ouch! Yeah, bitch! Yes, I'm awake!" screamed Gaya pain. Kelly let go.

"Well, what now. Where we are going and more importantly, we listen to Vaela?"

They looked at each other a little scared, but decided to go and walked out of the castle into a field. It bordered a bridge leading to a forest. Kelly decided nothing of pulling everything and looked at Gaya cheerfully as if nothing had happened. Gaya had tears in her eyes and looked at Kelly through her tears angrily. Angry because she was in pain and also because Kelly pulled from nowhere.

"What?" Kelly asked innocently as she walked across the bridge. But soon they were distracted again; when she bent over the railing, she looked bright but purple water of the river Lacrazitos.

"Aaahhhh!" screamed Kelly. Instead of seeing herself, she saw the face of a fearful mermaid, completely stretched and drained, like mascara. It seemed like the face anxiously called for help. But then the face disappeared. Kelly looked frightened! Gaya came running.

"What happened?" She cried.

"Nothing," stammered Kelly, she saw her own face in the water.

"Just tell me," Gaya insisted.

"N-no nothing," Kelly said.
"Well then, where are you going?"

"In any case, not that woods. Let's go through the castle, to the entrance where we met the giant with the V-door," Kelly stuttered a bit after. They ran quickly to the castle. Kelly wanted to be as far away from that river. Gaya did not understand it.

Quarrel

Kelly hobbled over the stones, while Gaya ate a sandwich to eat and was crumbling on Latrez's back.

Kelly sighed. She wanted to ask if she can have a sandwich. When she's at Lily's back, Lily would crumble and immediately flip. Latrez liked everything that Gaya did on top of her. Gaya herself was always so well equipped with everything and anything; piles of sweets, sandwiches, and pies, even sprouts did not missed her bag. Last night Gaya was even eating marshmallows.

"Gaya may I have a sandwich?" Kelly asked cautiously. Gaya looked up from the ground, smacking she asked, "Why?"
"I'm hungry," Kelly said with a squeaky voice, and her stomach growled so loudly that the birds flew out of the tree next to her.

"I can't hear it, sorry, I have nothing left."

"Amehoela," Kelly snapped suddenly, she was shocked.

"What?!" Gaya scowled at her and jumped off Latrez.

"Go get some yourself! At Merfitchy! There you are far away from me! Find your own food! I'm fed up! You always let me search for all the food, put it in my bag, do lugging, and you?! You packed your full and let me lug everything back! Why don't you peel a shrimp?" Gaya said insulted and ate a bun.

"Oh, whatever?!" shouted Kelly, "you let me do all the dirty work and pay for scary things. I always warn you somewhere before or rescue again!" Kelly pressed her index finger against her stomach so hard that she was quite stark white. Meanwhile, she grabbed her scratch pad and began wildly to draw, made the drawing into a wad and threw it at the hard road and counted to three.

She went on: "And Ella almost killed you! Accidentally, but yeah, but what did I do? I risked my life for you! And I cannot even get a stupid sandwich? Never mind! I'll just sit back. I'll ask Kafut Blue Bloods how to return home. I've had it with you and with all...!" screamed Kelly.

"Silent, I hear something..." Gaya said if she had not heard the rattle of her angry girlfriend.

Still arguing?

One Vaela

"That's the Gichi block that you hear buzzing. Vaela is calling. Well that's a long time since she called us," said Gaya. They reached the Gichi both with an annoyed face out of their pocket. The screen came with zzzz sound from the block. Gaya opened the Gichi. Kelly was uncertain and asked: "Do you have it open?"

"Sure." Vaela came with a rigorous but also cheerful face on the screen.

"Good and bad done girls. I cannot say more, "her face fell," and Sascha..."

"Sorry, but we had to really do it. She was very strong." muttered Gaya.

"Listen Vaela! You sometimes wish that we were caught?" said Kelly snappy.

Vaela looked sad. "Of course not dude! You think I'm like Ellegor?"

"No," said Kelly, "but how can it be? From all this I still believe nothing, I... I... don't dream? "She looked questioningly at Gaya.

"No Kelly!" Cried Vaela, "You cannot stop! Ellegor's too dangerous!" Vaela nearly bulged out of the screen.

"But still… 1… 2… 3… 3 questions!" Kelly counted on her fingers.

"Bring it on," winked Vaela.

"Why did I just now Jenny, and Gaya Choenitzy now? Is that a sign?"

"Listen," Vaela said in a whisper, "You have been chosen to be the saviors of Valariru! Kel, you have the power of the heat, or I will say fire. Jenny is a snake that spits fire, well, not yet, but later they will bring flames to hell and heaven. Gaya, your strength is ice, coolness, and Choenitzy is... I'll just say, a kingfisher. What was it again? Kel, visit Mobic."

Kelly grabbed her purse from the wooden box and pulled the phone out.

"Sasha has already said what species they are, but I don't believe her, so we need to check." Gaya said.

"Well, type in: 'Kingfisher' maybe you'll find something," Vaela said, nodding. Kelly tapped it in. This came to be:

Among the kingfishers include these types: The ice-iron Valariruse, Chaans the Valariruse kingfisher and Ijcha. The Ijcha and Valariruse kingfisher are the most frightened, but the most powerful and also the largest. The Ijcha is about 3 and a half feet, and the Valariruse kingfisher is just about 3 meters. They may very well fly, create icicles, live in icy regions and very icy that they can make so much like an avalanche, but beware, this is fatal. Only Ellegor can stand it!

"Choeny is among the best! Yup! Long live the Valariruse kingfisher!" Gaya jump around.

"Enough information," Kelly clicked it shut and hid it. "No!" Said Vaela, "what does it say to you?" Kelly typed 'fire hose' and looked what came to be:

Under the fire hoses are these species: The Fairsaing, the Fure Snake and the Fire Night. (The Fire Night is also called the South Valariruse Magaarninaz). The Fire Night and Fairsaing are the strongest. The Fairsaing is stronger, and is a bit bigger, but with a little more power. The Fire of Night are equally strong. The specialty of the Fairsaing is speed, as he is fast such that he can create a fire tornado and it happened to everyone in the neighborhood.

The specialty of the Fire Night is Nortsjaan. Which goes like this: he wags his tail in circles, so there is a huge fireball, he crawls in it, and spits fire to the extent that he sometimes be higher than himself. The Fire Night can grow from 3 to 5 meters, not higher, that simply does not exist. The Fairsaing is as much as 6 to 7 meters sometimes. But their fire could be higher than 2 kilometers. Sometimes it can even touch the sky and hell. It has even become a saying in Valariru.

Oo, yeah, there we were, he turns around, spits fire in the sphere, and so there is an explosion. Nobody survives this, only Ellegor and those who are destined to saviors or liberators of the sample of Valariru..

"Vaela would you know what will happen to Jenny?" Kelly hoping for a Fairsaing but a Fire Night is also good. Or they called her but just a South Valariruse Magaarninaz.

"May I see her here?" Vaela's head hovered in the air and the Gichi danced up and down. Kelly opened her bag and Jenny crept out.

"This is she,"... said Kelly. "Mmm... she is... I believe, yes, she is, yes! I'm sure...

Vaela nodded, "She is a Fire Night!"

"Yes!" cried Kelly. Then Sasha surely was right, "said Gaya.

"Yes," murmured Kelly,

"You must now go back," said Vaela and wanted to leave.

"No, wait!" cried Kelly, "I had two questions. How can we go home? And how can we beat Ellegor?" asked Kelly.

"When Ellegor defeated, you will automatically go home. You have to do anything for it."

"But how are we supposed to beat Ellegor then?" asked Gaya.

"So if we cannot beat him, we're never going home?" stammered Kelly.

"No, I'm afraid not," was the reply.

"But you also went very easy with the Jooki home anyway?"

"Yes, but this is your destiny, you know it now don't you?" Vaela sighed. They looked at each other blankly, as if they did not know how to deal with this answer.

"Yippee! What lucky sods we are," Gaya turned her eyes.

"But we have used it once! And then it worked well."

"For what?" Vaela took her eyebrow.

"In order to come up on a mountain..." Kelly said.

"Yup! But it is here, to go back home you cannot. Moreover, it cannot bring more than 100 kilometers away. Now I go, bye."

The Gichi clattered to the floor. Kelly picked it up and put it in her pocket.

"Shall we go?" Gaya looked at Kelly questioningly.

"All right, we're looking for an apartment or so and will just sit there. We'll see what happens... I need to rest."

A great hotel with a small apartment

Kelly and Gaya got a big white hotel inside. The doors opened with no sound. The hotel looked brand new. They walked to the counter, but there was none. "Press that bell," Gaya pointed to a small golden bell that was on the counter, ready to be used. Kelly shook it. A lady in a white suit was at the door.

"What can I do for you?" asked the woman. It was a Halloja. She was slim and had big dark green cat eyes. Her hands were like human hands but her ears were pointed. She was dark brown and when she smiled, Gaya saw that her teeth were white and glistening as sharp as her ears, her hair was dark and curly. It hung on the ground, as long as it was.

"We would like to rent an apartment," Kelly said. "Ahaahh... come with me, uh... how much you want to spend? Sorry, I just have to hire over 200 Celsia for two." Kelly and Gaya looked at each other happily, she nodded.

"We give 225 Celsia for two." She gave the woman 225 Celsia.

"I will show you the way to the apartment." She walked out of the hotel and came on a narrow path. There was a small white house with a small balcony. "Awesome," said Kelly, and Halloja let them inside. The apartment was great. Not so big, but clean and nice. A big hotel with a small apartment. They sat down on the bed and slept all day, they were so tired.

To rest

Kelly got out of bed. She slid into her slippers. With tired eyes, she looked around, it was late in the morning. She walked to the balcony door and opened it. The bright light blinded her for a moment, but then she saw all happy living crocuses, snowdrops and daffodils. They laughed at her cheerfully, that was a nice feeling. In her slippers she shuffled carefully with small steps downwards. The grass was dry and green. She looked down and wriggled her feet.

"Are you bent?" Kelly leaned forward

"Yes, someone kicked his heel on me," replied the narcisje with a squeaky voice.

"Will you take me?" Kelly picked the narcisje and ran up the stairs back up to the balcony. She opened the door and then went straight to the small kitchen. She grabbed a glass from the cupboard and filled it up with water. Kelly stuck the narcisje in it.

"Thank you very much," said the narcisje grateful, "I don't know what would have happened if..."

At that moment a sleeping and tired Gaya came inside.

"Haaah... Hatsie! What are you doing?" She ran her hand along her nose.

"Nothing, this narcisje was trampled, I picked her, are you cold?" Kelly poured a glass of apple juice for Gaya.

"I don't know, I'm... Hatsie! A little allergic to daffodils, I believe."

"Mmmm..." muttered Kelly, and held the narcisje Gaya's eyes. But she did not sneeze.

"That is not so," muttered Kelly again. The narcisje writhed up and down and said in a squeaky voice: "Allergic? For a daffodil? That cannot be! What nonsense!"

"What will it be?" Kelly looked around whether there was anything else that Gaya may be allergic to. Maybe Jenny? Whether she was suddenly allergic to Latrez and Lily? Or Choenitzy!

Kelly looked at Gaya, "where is Choeny?"

"Still in the bedroom. To rest or so."

Kelly ran to the bedroom and saw Choenitzy lying on the bed. "Choeny! Choenitzy! Wake up,"

Kelly grabbed the animal and patted on the head, "come with me. I need you." She ran with Choenitzy in her arms to Gaya. "Is this it?" Kelly pointed her index finger at the still half asleep Choenitzy.

"No!" Cried Gaya. She just Choenitzy and it was already a treasure that she could not miss. Kelly kept the animal for Gaya. She sneezed not. No Ha, Gaya said that she was not allergic to candy and especially for drop, because then Kel would have eaten everything.
"Shall we continue? This stay here pleases me, but I want to go home. Gaya, the faster we beat Ellegor the better, and the sooner we can go home, right?" asked Kelly.

"Exactly," confirmed Gaya. Kelly already ran to the bathroom to shower. Moments later she was back and was already fully dressed.

"Well, are you ready Gaya?" They drew their shoes and coat and walked Lily and Latrez out. Jenny sat on Kelly's shoulder and Choenitzy sat as an eagle at Gaya's shoulder. They walked a long way. Until a miracle happened.

The change

Jenny slid to the ground and Choenitzy sat down on the ground. Jenny's cute little head turned into a large cup. Her eyes seemed to bulge out of her head. They were nice and big purple. Her slender little snake body turned into a gigantic snake's body of 3 meters! Wait... he grew still.

"This... this... cannot... they are still only 3 mm gauge," stammered Kelly.

Her tongue that occasionally slipped out, became thicker and bigger, and the gap between her tongue was very big! The tips of her tongue seemed to be sharper and longer. The tip of her tail also changed and there were rings. Just like Ella had them. They continued to grow... And then Kelly saw that her body was greater than 3 meters.

"Choeny" cried Gaya and grabbed her anxious face. While Jenny's body turned into a huge yellow with light blue body, her eyes were so big and beautiful, as yet no one had ever seen, and Choenitzy grew.

Choenitzy's three tufts on its head grew longer. Her beak was crooked and her silvery wings. The feathers all stood forward. Her beak was bigger and more curved. Her little legs that could not even break a snail's shell, large claws and her nails sharp as knives. Her beak was as crooked as her nails. Then something happened scary, front, somewhere far below her chin. At the bottom of her body, in front, came suddenly legs, which were bigger, bigger, until a leg was fixed. So it happened that Choenitzy had four legs! With large claws with long nails, each creature could tear.
Choenitzy and Jenny had evolved into adult animals. "My great Jenny! What has she grown?" Kelly ran to her 'tube'.

"Great! You have evolved!" exclaimed Kelly.

"My Choenitzy..." Gaya rushed to Choenitzy. "Woow. Those are only warriors! Terrifying creatures! Horror beasts! Well, then, dear horror beasts. This is cool!" exclaimed Kelly and scribbled on Jenny.

"Can you really fly Choeny? High? Far?" Gaya asked and they balanced on Choenitzy 'wings to get on top of her.

"Can you spit fire?" Kelly noticed that Jenny was still coming smattering hard and stood in front of her face as big as their first apartment. "You're really greater than 3 meters! Ehh... 1, 2,3,4,5... 5 feet so I treasure! Yeah day! 7 meters! Spit fire," Kelly rattled on.

Jenny coughed and said: "I can talk better, ehh... off," she spat out a small fire.

"Come on," Kelly shook her head, "you can do better than this? Come on! Spit! Spit! Let yourself go!" Jenny coughed again, opened her mouth wide open and spat. A flame of 9 meters shot out of her mouth. Kelly was black.

"Good," said and fell backwards. Jenny sucked moment, then slid her tongue out of her mouth.

"My mouth feels hot," said the snake. "That makes sense," said Gaya, "you breathed fire, hello. Duh! Sense that you have a hot mouth." Kelly rose with difficulty, shook back and forth and she was no longer black.

"Perfect," she said, "that's what I mean."

"Now you," Gaya scrambled from Choenitzy and looked her straight in the eye. "Do icicles," she said.

"Then I pierce you, Choenitzy said doubtfully." Choenitzy got his eyebrow and mouth on.

"So, do just ice."

"Good," Choenitzy blew a wave of coolness flowed through Gaya go.

"Good, good," she said, "and now ice, not air, okay?"

"I'll try." Choenitzy made a strange breathing sound, especially because Gaya was immediately frozen. "Woow!" exclaimed Kelly, "now you Jen, do your job." Jenny blew a flame and hit the ice. Whoosh, everything was at a glance away. Gaya was thawed. Everything worked perfectly.

"Now look at that stupid Ellegor! He cannot stop us! With such great beasts!" cried Kelly.

"Awesome!" cried Gaya, and the horses, the new Jenny and Choenitzy, walked away.

Horse Shit and disco der Eden Disappearing

"Great grits!" exclaimed the Halloja. Kelly and Gaya arrived at the desk and reported that they were leaving and that Jenny and Choenitzy had grown.

"Really?" asked the Halloja.

"Yes," Gaya nodded, "we really have gone. Our horses are probably waiting for the door, she had let a little dazed by farts and poo so we had them for the door, lol," Kelly said.

They walked out of the hotel. With their first day apartment they were happy, but it was unfortunately over again; they must surely beat Ellegor. Suddenly, all the people ran away screaming from the hotel. Kelly and Gaya grabbed their nose.
"According to me Lily and Latrez done their daily needs, and not just a little bit Kelly, Blimey! What a stink..." Gaya said with pinched nose.

"Yes, let Lily and Latrez take before someone gets very angry." Kelly said in a voice like a potato was in her throat, "hopefully no more it stinks there, and no one is going to stick their..." said Kelly and turned her eyes.

Gaya, jumped on Latrez jumped and rode away. Kelly rode behind her, green, sick head.

Kelly stepped off Lily. "Gaya," she whispered, "where we are now."

"Somehow, we'll ask you?" Gaya said, frowning and stepped from Latrez. "Well, there is a kind of flat, and we can ask," Kelly fixed Lily to a pole while Gaya did also the same with Latrez. When she walked into the apartment, they all immediately saw people dancing to deafening music. Gaya and Kelly immediately took to their ears. It looked like a violin scratched as the voice of Sascha, and a voice that sounded like a bad singer with toothache. Kelly looked like she had to surrender and make fallow sounds.

"Well not to exaggerate," said Gaya.

"What?!" Kelly shouted over the music, "I can't hear you!"

"I said, not to exaggerate," Gaya tried again.

"I cannot understand! What should I write? Kelly roared back.

They signaled each other by walking until they came to an enormous glass staircase that led to a small private room with lots of glass. They walked with their hands to their ears pressed up the stairs to the room. Kelly knocked on the door. A small plump woman opened the door. She had grayish spiky hair that stuck out in all directions. Ears as big as kites, fingers as long as pencils, her little mouth with scary witch but two teeth were straight forward. And brown eyes that were reminiscent of a button on a remote control, so small. Her pointy stick - which was clasped by her pencil fingers - dangling beside her 5 millimeters long leg. (Figuratively, though.) She pushed her stick against Kelly's belly, and chided cranky, "What?!" Her mouth stood down from her throat and there came a muffled beep sound.

Gaya turned her eyes impatiently. Kelly pushed back the stick with her index finger. "Excuse me," she said irritably, "ehh... we wanted to ask where exactly we are ehh... namely... pretty much... just a little... lost..." said Kelly, a little shy.

"Aaahh," there appeared a smile around her little chapped mouth, "lost... come in and be welcome in the Disco der Eden Disappear!"

Gaya and Kelly thoughtfully walked inside the glass room. They did that well understood? Disco of... what?

Kelly pretended she was not afraid and said "sorry, but uh... are you a... Halloja?"

"No, I'm a Vatty," replied the woman.

114

"They see there are also some different?" Asked Kelly surprised, "and they are not all equally friendly?"

"I? Yes that look different, yes, but you guys know where you are? Are not you a little frightened... or do you just pretending? "The woman asked impatiently.

The Vatty took a huge swig from a square high cup with scary terrifying animal heads painted on. "No," boasted Gaya, "why should we be afraid? Because a disco has such a weird name? Besides, everything seems really together... the Chanana's... the Zodiac..." Gaya tried again to divert the scary woman.

"What?!" interrupted the Vatty She put the cup with a bang next to her on a small table.

"Just don't! Animals... Chanana's forces...... nature... trees... don't you see that it is all very different!" Shrieked the Vatty out. She was clearly offended.

"Different?" Gaya took her right eyebrow. "Yes, exactly," interrupted Kelly Gaya, "I see nothing here that is different from the ordinary world. Except... the trees, and the animals that live...... which are very different and can talk... and Chanana's... errr... and the..."Kelly saw the Vatty grinned and quickly looked the other way whistling. "Well... that's quite little ehhh...?" Muttered Kelly still implausible.

"You babble but what, bunch of stupid girls! Anyway, I'm Giralla, the Vatty of Disappearing Ones! And you are? "

"Kelly," Gaya pointed to Kelly, "and I am Gaya."

"Gaya and Kelly? Aha... well, well..." She chuckled and rubbed her hands.

"You are at the Hotel-where-you-will-remain eternal."

"Hotel where...?" Gaya said shakily.

"What be-do-you referring to that? Because... that's very kind of you... we will not stay here forever though."

The Vatty chuckled again and said: "Well, we'll see you again, everyone who has been in the disco, will never be able to leave...! For who once this terrible loud music is heard, will be infected and cannot leave! "Shrieked the woman hatefully.

The girls looked at each other shocked at what they had to put with the crazy Vatty crazy. Kelly cleared all courage and said: "Well, uh, we'll go again eh, nice to meet you but eh... we try to briefly dancing in the disco okay? Bye!"

They walked away in a hurry, the mad woman behind, the Vatty tolerated it because she knew they would never be able to leave. Gaya and Kelly walked through the crowd, their ears pressed with their hands. And who were suddenly there? Their boyfriends Choenitzy and Jenny!
"Oh, how wonderful, you come when called!" cried Gaya happy.

"Kel, I have an idea! Choeny, do your thing, that means, blow as hard as you can in the disco and let everyone but a minute cool down, including impaired Vatty, because they are all mad here!"

Choenitzy was excited and blew as hard as she could, and what happened? "WOW, Choeny, look what you've done! Everything and everyone frozen! Okay, friends, we can move forward again, haha, you've done your best brave Choeny, you get a big kiss!" That Gaya had better not do, because now she was stuck in quite as icy Choenitzy.

"Oh Gaya, not so smart, so now I have to ask Jenny or ask if she wants to give you a lick, then you melted so again."

So to get used to their new big friends. But luckily they could now go further. The contamination of the music had not worked, so they were not forever stuck in that crazy 'Hotel-where-you-will-remain eternal' and Disco Der Disappearing Ones, thanks Jenny and Choenitzy!

The voice

Kelly and Gaya and sat quietly on the backs of their horses, still enjoying a bit after their victory.

Tick, tock, tick, tock. Soft raindrops fell on the little stones. Becoming more and louder until it became a downpour.

"No, do you? Just now!" Gaya said angrily. "Just leave," Kelly said quietly, "yet does not matter? Grab a piece of candy and let the rain."

Gaya angrily pulled on the reins of Latrez and gestured to her to stop. She hurled the bag off her back and fumbled in her purse when she caught a wet bag of candy.

"What?!" she shouted excitedly. "No waterproof bag so, clever of you," grinned Kelly.

"Shut up," murmured Gaya. Kelly grabbed a piece of paper from her pocket and scribbled a drawing. She folded it up, gave it to Gaya and pulled Lily's rein to say that she did anything had to ride harder. Angrily Gaya folded the paper. There was a girl, apparently Kelly; with slit eyes, she stuck out her tongue. Gaya stuffed the little drawing up and threw it as far as they could go. Brat thought Gaya.

She galloped with an angry face behind Kelly; but when she was almost at her Gaya suddenly heard a terrifying voice: "away go away you should not be here. Go with Kelly and the horses, or something terrible will happen to you. More she did not hear. Frankly, they did not want to hear more.

"What is it Gaya?" Kelly stood beside her, "you look pale."

"Ehh... nothing though."

"Well, tell me."

"There is nothing! Come on, let's go," Gaya stuck her chin in the air and drove off.

Kelly turned her eyes, and went to her but just - sigh - chasing. But did not see that Gaya looked pale as a white downy feather.

The letter

"What are you saying to me? Did you hear a voice? Voice of scary? Or voice of fun?"

"No voice of strange and that gives you the chills." Gaya said.

"Strange? Chills? "Kelly raised an eyebrow.

"Leave it. I become irritable and you don't believe me."

"Good, good," Kelly grinned "but remember that if you have something like that again, or rather hear a voice, tell me!" And she thought that you saw on her face. They decided to drive.
Suddenly blew a note against Kelly's face:

"Huh! Gaya! Do you have turned off the light?" Gaya snatched the paper from Kelly's head and looked grumpy for.
"
Oh," muttered Kelly, "excuse me."

Gaya read the paper carefully in themselves. "What does it say?" Kelly tried to read it but Gaya held the paper right in front of her head so Kelly could not see it.

"3 Hours at night-," was the only piece that Gaya read aloud.

"What? What?!"Kelly asked impatiently and snatched the paper from Gaya's hands. She read aloud:

To: Kelly and Gaya.

Coming here is like planting trees; easy and sometimes difficult, in your case it was apparently easy so far. But going back will be more difficult, at least alive.

You have you lost contact with Vaela and asking for help is impossible. Come to the Valariru Nachtegaalplein in Voelaanze 3 o'clock at night! Or else.

If you won't come, you can only dream... do you understand what I mean?!

"What?!" bellowed Gaya. "From whom is this stupid letter, of Ellegor?! Is this guy crazy or something, what a bizarre language he used, and at 3 o'clock at night?!"

"Is that guy really crazy or something?" cried Kelly.

"Apparently." Gaya threw the paper on the floor, jumped and Latrez stamped on it with all the power and fury on the paper.

"Well, well keep stamping like no Chanana or man ever did," sighed Kelly.

"And why are you so sure?" Gaya looked into her eyes. "Therefore," snapped Kelly, "and shut up, or the stapler goes to work and will you just shut up."

"Haha, very funny, and if that does not work, he should loose wires above!" Taunted Gaya back.

Kelly stamped her feet on the ground. "Cannot, I just have no brains and wires in my head," Kelly continued.

"Keep well Kelly, we look who sent this scary letter, better than that stupid bickering between us, right?"

"Good idea," muttered Kelly, "they can graze us immediately to take," she began.

"Keep your head now!" Gaya said pissed. "I am fed up! Now let's see where this is stupid Valariru Nachtegaalplein. "Kelly and Gaya got on their horses and rode on their way.

Alarm!

Kelly yawned. "I'm so tired, boy!"

"Are you serious? Hello, "Gaya waved her hand in front Kelly's face," we must go to the plaza remember?"

"Duh," Kelly turned with her big green eyes," you thought I had forgotten that?"

Gaya left her flat horizontal hand down her neck. "You start again so unkind, and I keep well to shut your mouth."

"Sorry Gaya."

"Ma'am, sir," Gaya held a lady and a gentleman on, "uh... you know sometimes where Valariru Nachtegaalplein is?"

"Yes, yes," the woman with a strange voice answered, she sounded like a squeaky mouse. "This street... and then left."

It was 10 to 3 at night, Kelly and Gaya were waiting as petrified, next to their horses, Jenny and Choenitzy. Gaya looked anxiously around.

"Would it have been a joke?"

"If so..." Kelly turned her hand a fist and hit it on her other hand, "the culprit is not one piece back on this strange planet of Valuriruse!"
"Shut up now anyway, I get the creeps. It is already so cold and scary here. You know, sometimes I think you're pretty scary Kel, nice, but scary," said Gaya in anguish.

"Well thank you for the compliment," said Kelly sarcastically, "but I want to hear, because our enemy is perhaps afraid of me! Come on, it's been 5 for 3, I wait 10 seconds and as smooth Janus there still is not, I 'm out," Kelly said.

Gaya was no longer listening and suddenly pointed straight ahead. "There is something..."

Kelly had suddenly scream of panic. "AHHHH! Was all but a bad dream or a bad joke... but alas! The alarm!"

The beginning of the end...

"Who are you...?" Stammered Gaya and stood paralyzed. There was a horrible-looking figure in the black for them, the man opened his hood down, and a scary headline appeared: he looked pale, basically white, with bulging eyes, an ugly skin and a crooked nose. His bulging eyes looked scary to them, he had a sly smile on his mouth, and his nostrils were larger and smaller with each snuff.

"Ellegor!" whispered Kelly.

"Exactly child... you guessed it, and I'll tell you something, your days are numbered!" he said softly and eerie tone. Then he took a small marble out and held it up to the light, so that the marble shone beautifully and was enlightened.

"Haha, you want to beat us with a marble? Are we marbles?" Kelly put her hands on her hips.

"That's what you wanted," whispered his hollow voice, which made them even more afraid.

"Okay, I grease him," said Gaya determined and wanted to run away, but Kelly grabbed her roughly by the arm.

"Are you crazy? We have toiled so hard, and all for nothing, right? Think of Ella, Vaela, to anyone who will be killed by Ellegor if we don't continue. Put your nerve on the side, we must persevere!" Kelly said on compelling but hushed tones. Gaya was almost crying. Kelly loosened her grip, her face was no longer angry and then she said, "Well, you stay here, I'm going to do it." She stepped confidently forward.

At that time Ellegor whispered very slowly and scary: "Vaarniaquyi" The marble suddenly became yellowish and a piece flew into the air, fell down again, then fell into a thousand pieces and cracking apart. A dazzling light then came out. Kelly looked with surprised at Gaya. There appeared a huge dragon, yellow green, from the marble.

Kelly clenched her fist. "Oh, you wanna play rough? Good! Jenny! Up to it!" Kelly pointed to Ellegor. Jenny rushed loud hissing at him.

"Mita, grab that violent and ugly reptile!" exclaimed Ellegor. The dragon went off to Jenny.

"Who is now violent here, and especially who is ugly here?! Chanana's take your power as taking slaves and finally murder? So what is not violent to it, you ugly monster?!" shouted Kelly heroic. "Jenny, wag your tail and bite him in his wings!"

Gaya was still petrified. Well, wait a minute, okay you Jenny, I Choenitzy! Gaya suddenly thought without fear. Then she screamed so loud she could: "CHOENITZY, beat your wings and let them your see!"

Choenitzy took action and did as he was commanded. He hit as hard as he could with his wings, and when the dragon seemed exhausted, he took a deep breath, blew hard, and there appeared a large ice ball that got bigger and bigger. Kelly looked at Gaya puzzled.

"That's the power of..."

"The BP?" Interrupted Kelly her grinning.

"Very funny," Gaya said irritably. "No, the power of Choenitzy!"

The ice ball had become gigantic and Choenitzy threw with all his strength against the ice ball Ellegor, which fell with a thump. When Choenitzy hit his wings and flew into the air, once high enough he let himself hurtling down. He had a stone in his claws and threw the rock hard down. Don't touch! At the head of the dragon. Kelly grabbed the marble and shouted: "Vaarniaqu, and then something else!"

"Vaarniaquyi back" improved Gaya.

"Vaarniaquyi back!"

If a miracle shrank the dragon and immediately went back into the marble. The crack in the strange green marble was whole again. Kelly stopped the fan with dragon and all solemnly in her pocket.

"So, that was just a breeze, strange that nobody comes back alive, you're a gentle breeze, Ellegor!"

"Easy? I? Don't mock the Almighty, you silly kids! You may have that stupid dragon. Because... I myself am too!"

He hit his hand under his coat, and pointed to Kelly and Gaya, who stood next to each other like two silly chickens were slaughtered so and roast. He mumbled something, so Kelly and Gaya suddenly back shots. They got a hollow feeling in their stomach, as if just a stone hard pruning had gone through her belly.

They rebounded like a slingshot against a rock and lay as motionless. When scrambled Gaya, SHE grabbed a large branch, held it, and hissed, "Ice."

The branch became cold, froze and eventually there was a huge layer of ice around it. Gaya screamed as loud as she could. Her hand shot a beam of ice, frozen pushed forward and landed in Ellegor's stomach. He flinched from the pain.
"Haha, it stands right now, eh, 1-1!"

Meanwhile Kelly was scrawled his feet and pointed to Ellegor. "Fire," she screamed, her hand shot a flame that Ellegor now struck against his shin, and caused a cut, as big as his entire leg. From the huge gash now seemed to burn a flame... Ellegor looked at it when he spoke something unintelligible and looked Gaya and Kelly withering.

"You're not there yet, stupid Hessel-girls, you really think I feel all this?" She looked at him in disbelief.

Then he threw a piece of chewing gum pink somewhere in the middle of the field and there was a huge bang place Kelly Gaya and flew into the air and came back a few meters further down. Gaya slammed into a tree and Kelly flew into the bushes. She got battered out of the bushes, carefully, in order not to get more scratches. Kelly Ellegor pointed out, they had a lot of pain and on her forehead dripped a trickle of blood.

"Jenny," she said exhausted while she took a huge thorn from her arm, "try the Nortsjaan." Jenny wagged her tail, a huge fireball appeared, and she crawled into it himself and spat as far as they could see the fireball. A direct hit, it hit Ellegor exactly on his heart. He fell down, tried again just to stand and then suddenly something very strange happened.

The heart of Ellegor turned into dust, and grit fell from his chest and then there was a hole in his chest! It did not look scary, but very crazy. There was no blood or so. Only a pile of debris on the ground. Then the same thing happened with his left leg. And when his left arm. Another pile of debris. Finally, very slowly to the bottom of its body. And half of his head.

"Noooo..." croaked Ellegor and looked at his crushed body. He said a spell, but it was inaudible.
Suddenly Kelly was all surrounded by electricity, it seemed like they were under power. Was this the end of her life?

Kelly tried to stay upright, but she could not, she fell to the ground. The electricity was gone, but she lay motionless on the ground.

"Haha! Your girlfriend is dead, no one survives my Electerbol. Valariru is the country where no one returns alive, that I had promised you?!" Grinned hideously Ellegor at Gaya.

"You forgot Ellegor..." Gaya stood up, still half crying, "that we are still here! Choenitzy! Do your ice burst! NOW!" Choenitzy flew into the air, crashed down and folded his wings together, just before the ground he folded his wings open and a giant ice eruption occurred.

Ellegor stopped, but as before now done what everyone hoped, the remaining parts of Ellegor also turned into dust!

When Kelly was back slowly. She had to smiles, Gaya equally wide. It was succeeded them! They walked slowly away, tired but happy. But what happened? The pile of debris formed together and then went up to them, they took slicing, and they fell with a thud on the ground and continued to lie. Motionless. And the pile of debris then disappeared into thin air.

The return trip

Kelly slowly opened her eyes, she felt sick and had pain everywhere. Where was she? She saw the seagulls flying above her in the clear air. Oh yes, she saw Lily and Latrez. She turned on her side. What a hard floor, and wet! She sat bolt upright. She looked beside him lay there Gaya and above her flew a bird. A very large. Oh, which was Choenitzy! Jenny swam beside her. She looked beside her, she saw water. Yes, they floated in a boat at sea. When she saw in gold letters: "Merfitchy." They were safe on the Merfitchy! But where was that creep of an Ellegor then?

"Gaya" Kelly whispered, shaking her violently together.

"What?" Gaya struggled to his feet.

"Where are we Kel, oh I have a pain in my head!" She sat up.

"We are on the Sweet Seas Valariru," said Kelly, "at least I. Faith" She stuck her finger in the water and licked it. Yes, pepper and lemonade, this was the Sweet Sea Valariru. She felt in her pocket, a marble. She looked at him intently. Green. Everything came back like a bad dream up.

Suddenly went off a beeping sound, the blue Gichi shot into the air. There appeared a face on a screen of the Gichi. Vaela! What a relief. Who was there, too. Kelly looked at her with big eyes, what she felt safe now!

"Very well done," said Vaela, "great! Ella is happy, everyone is freed. Ellegor is dead. Well done, great job girls!"

"But, I still remember..." began Kelly questionable.

"Shhh, quiet but Kelly, the grit of Ellegor is also gone," Vaela said.

"Yeah, okay, but I did not ask, I..."

"It's good Kelly, and yes, you may go home."

"But... are you there, you go with us?" Kelly had forgotten what she wanted to say, because it struck her suddenly inside, Vaela had to go!

"Yes, I'm coming," winked Vaela.

"But your parents are here, all the way from the Netherlands came here, Netherlands is very far away from Asia, nice of them huh that they have come. That proves that they really want to know how you, but I've said that all is well!"

What delicious, on the way home, gosh, what they wanted to say that, to Miu, the cat, and Angel, the other cat and of course their dog Bora. And their parents remember. The parents of Kelly and Gaya would be so happy to see them again, and of course vice versa.

Gaya swallowed by an English licorice, "Hey, we're going home!"

Gaya and dog Bora

First a party!

The Merfitchy was set aside. There were heaps of people on the side. As a true victors they got off the boat along with LILY and Latrez, Jenny and Choenitzy after it. Upon seeing Jenny and Choenitzy recoiled backward anyone. "Calm down!" Gaya called to the crowd, "they can't do a thing!"

The people took a sigh of relief. At the end of the procession were the parents of Kelly Gaya and waiting, they had tears in their eyes and joy to the right, next to the parents of Gaya, was Vaela. She smiled and gave a big wink.

When she stepped on a stage that was pretty high. Arm in arm with their kids were the parents of Gaya and Kelly watch Vaela.

"First I want to say that Kelly and Gaya are the first to be returned alive from Valariru! So give them a warm welcome applause!" Vaela could hardly at the microphone, so small she was. Everyone cheered so hard, who was still in the town itself and was not on the shore, has certainly thought that there was a hand grenade exploded. When the weather was still Vaela continued, "and they have brought something alive, a Valariruse-kingfisher, and a Fire Night! Or also a South Valariruse Magaarninaz! JENNY AND CHOENITZY!"

The great beasts came forward and everyone watched breathlessly. Then, very slowly, they did their head up and spit; Jenny came a flame. To the sky, it seemed. And Choenitzy came a huge icicle, which reached as high as the flame Jenny. Everyone cheered in admiration. The horses were then also come on stage, who one by one received a thunderous applause, and each horse received a ribbon around their necks.

Kelly and Gaya got as much such a heavy medal that she could hardly bear their necks.
"And now I want..." but at that moment Vaela stumbled over her shoelace and fell off the stage. Everyone was just the shock of their lives; Vaela changed because, while they fell in a small pitch-black cat. With

golden eyes. She came up on her feet. Then she pushed her legs forward and suddenly she changed lightning fast back into a human.

She coughed, "Yeah, uh... well, now I want Laicha here!" People looked incredulously at Vaela who pretended nothing had happened.

She stepped on stage again, followed by Laicha. Laicha coughed, then said softly from embarrassment, "ehh... I've caught Serge with a gadget that I've ever gotten from Vaela, he is, uh... caught, and he's gone."

It was just completely silent, then again, there was a huge cheer, and everyone who had a cap tossed him in the air. Vaela smiled broadly, she was so happy that she took a run, dived off the stage and changed again in the black cat. She meowed as hard as she could. Kelly and Gaya were so happy and relieved and started merry dance on the big party and then everyone started to celebrate. There were snacks. The party lasted until late at night. Then they took leave of their parents, who again already left for the Netherlands.

Home again!

Two days later Kelly Gaya and also went back home, with Vaela as cat -Choenitzy, Jenny, and LILY Latrez. It was a long but pleasant journey.

"Hey, uh... UAE! Will you stay with us? "Gaya asked when they finally arrived home. Vaela beamed, pushed off and when she was a little person.

"Oh please," she said, "my parents don't live here, of course, so I have no home here, I slept like cat always among the rubbish. But I was like cat always much happier as a person. As a child I was terribly spoiled with all the toys that I wanted and had a very large bedroom, but it did not make me happy though! But if cat I was free and I had a lot of boyfriends. Between the garbage so. Very convenient, but dirty. You find at least, right? "

"That's why you did not want to talk about..." muttered Gaya.

"Jekkie" said Kelly "cat or not, I will never be able to sleep between the garbage! I'm not crazy! No cats girl, but you come live with us. "

"But Vaela, how do you always knew where we were? You always sent notes, "said Gaya.

"Yes," winked Vaela, "but I can also turn into a cat? So why could I not? "

"Oh, okay, well, you don't need to give away all your secrets. Enough asked, let's now our cats and our dog see you. And want to help Jenny and Choenitzy by pushing the house to the backyard? We don't garden entrance, "Kelly said.

"Yeah, sure, why not? They must also live, seen only in the outdoors, "said Vaela. They pushed the animals through the house out into the garden. A pair of vases and cabinets fell at that, but yes, maybe Vaela could though refurbishing moment... and then there were no more tables but gadget boxes. Better still.

Vaela jump tables - but as cat - and played anywhere. Even with the wool. It was evening, and Kelly and Gaya were eating to make while Vaela (as a man) was watching TV.

"Are not you tired UAE?" Asked Kelly, "You're in for quite a while."

"Cats go to bed when they want, Kel."

"Oh, yeah forget. But tell now know who or what you are exactly! "Kelly asked curiously.

"I'm into my second year raised by cats. Then I got a drink, so I would always be female, but my parents were moving cats, and left me, because they were the people forced to go along. I said I'd save myself, but it was difficult as cats without parents. As a little girl, Esther, found me and gave me to her parents, she first wanted to not like me, but when it, when I was two years old. From that moment I was so raised by people, so I'm half man, half cat. You call that a Cat-Man."

"Sounds scary, but I would really have liked to be such a Cat-Man," said Gaya.

"Yeah, me too," said Kelly, "you nice limber, and you still have nine lives, and you can still change, convenient say! And uh... anyway Gaya, you have those Laicha and her family all called to thank? "Tried Kelly.

"Excuse me, can you do that also," said Gaya nipping.

"Excuse me, excuse me, did not know you were angry," continued Kelly.

She turned on the tap and kept a pot of sprouts under. "Brussels sprouts?" Vaela shot up from the couch, "sorry, but why dirty sprouts?" She jumped nimbly over the couch and looked Kelly and Gaya with big eyes.

"Can we eat sprouts? Lusts you that? "Gaya asked incredulously. Kelly laughed, "No of course not!"

134

"But why are you that sprouts washing and Gaya cook a sauce?" Kelly laughed even harder, she almost dropped her hands from the pan.

"We cook it for our own cats, Jenny, Choenitzy, LILY and Latrez! They love sprouts," Kelly said proudly. "Oh," sighed Vaela "strange that they see good and I don't, I'm still a cat? Sometimes, at least. "

"What we eat then?" Vaela asked curiously.

"Cauliflower" Gaya said keen. They had indeed everything. Kelly stuck her tongue out, "not really pull in today."

"Why do you eat it? If you are without parents you doing good what do you want? "Asked Vaela.
"Yes, that was the intention of living alone, but we have a calendar when we exactly what to eat, that our parents have made. Stupid huh? Every night they call us whether we have really eaten what was on the calendar. "Vaela laughed it.

"What is so funny?" Asked Kelly also half laughing. Gaya also burst out laughing, the three of them got the giggles.

"Hahahahaha! Well, come, we will cauliflower delicious food, "said Gaya.

CPSIA information can be obtained at www.ICGtesting.com
Printed in the USA
BVOW08s2316210616

452931BV00001BA/36/P